I0556176

Crazy Little Thing Called Love

A touching, heartwarming story that takes your breath away.

Characters that will have you feeling so many emotions. It deals with family, misunderstandings, ranch life, horses, life long love and of course Pumpkin the cat.

Tony and Sophia's story had me laughing, crying and a bit frustrated with them at times. To me that is good writing when I can be moved to so many emotions while reading . The story is so good, I couldn't put it down.

- B

With This Heart

Such a sweet heartwarming romance about second chance love between two people who are obviously meant to be together. You won't want to put this story down until you're finished reading.

This is a wonderful series. Those of you who love military romance, wounded warrior romance and romantic suspense will love the stories written by this super talented, fabulous author!

– TAMMY

Maggie's Revenge

The first comment I can easily make here is: MAGGIE'S REVENGE punched my 'WOW' button!

Magdalena Holt goes rogue and deep undercover for the DEA... Fast forward: > Olga, a once teenage prostitute, and four others are captured by 'sex traffickers', put in a 'mud pit' basement. After several attempts, beatings, torture, and a lot of action, the group of five make their escape...

The suspense is staggering as 'Maggie' and her tattered and broken group valiantly withstand the vagaries of the Mexican compound and hell-hole, escape, and then await the DEA to recover them. Maggie wants to get home and bring down the most evil man she has ever known...a criminal and terrifying clown named Chenglei.

The romantic component in this exciting novel involves Maggie's partner and agency member, Adam O'Connor, who the boss fears will jeopardize rescue efforts because he is 'too close' - with his feelings for Maggie.

MAGGIE'S REVENGE is masterfully written and a 'must read' for the 'mystery and suspense' book lovers! The novel would also make a great movie! It's been a while since I've seen this 'theme' in movies...of course, I only watch an occasional TV movie.

- JULIE GEHRANDT

SKATING ON THIN ICE

THE MEN OF WARHAWKS- BOOK 1

JACQUIE BIGGAR

WAVEFRONT PUBLISHING

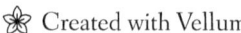 Created with Vellum

As a proud Canadian, I would like to dedicate this book to our hockey heroes- past and present.

Hockey is not a one-man show; it's a team effort. If you don't work as a team - even if one or two guys aren't working - you're not going to win. That's the way it is.

- GUY LAFLEUR

CONTENTS

Introduction	xiii
Preface	xv
Chapter 1	1
Chapter 2	7
Chapter 3	13
Chapter 4	18
Chapter 5	24
Chapter 6	31
Chapter 7	37
Chapter 8	47
Chapter 9	53
Chapter 10	61
Chapter 11	70
Chapter 12	78
Chapter 13	86
Chapter 14	92
Chapter 15	101
Chapter 16	107
Chapter 17	116
Chapter 18	121
Chapter 19	127
Chapter 20	134
Chapter 21	141
Chapter 22	150
Chapter 23	159

Preview Tempted by Mr. Wrong   163
Free Download!   169
Afterword   171
Acknowledgments   173
About the Author   175
Also by Jacquie Biggar   177

Will a killer accomplish the greatest hat trick of his career?

Sam Walters has made a deal with the devil. In order to win a much-needed contract as physical therapist to one of the NHL's leading hockey teams, she must delay the recovery of their sniper, Mac Wanowski. The trouble is, the more she gets to know the taciturn hockey player, the more she aches to help him.

Mac 'The Hammer' Wanowski has chased the Stanley Cup dream for too many years. Last time he was close it cost him his wife. As injuries continue to plague the team, Mac works to catch a killer and keep the woman he's come to love from the hands of a madman.

Hockey can be a dangerous sport, especially when millions of dollars are at stake.

Sam removed a full container of eggs, a tomato, an onion, a bright yellow banana pepper, and a block of cheddar cheese from the refrigerator and used her butt to close the door. She juggled her armload past the cat and dumped it on the granite countertop. "Okay, Cleo, your turn." She stooped to scratch her between the ears, then returned to the fridge. "Does Dad give you milk, hmm?" The carton was in the door, the seal broken, so she gave it a sniff before deigning it good enough for her new four-footed friend. A quick search of the pantry later and Cleo the cat was daintily eating her dinner, ears flicking at every little sound.

Sam frowned. How long did it take to start a fire? Maybe Mac was taking his time so she'd do the cooking. Not happening. She wandered down the hall, expecting to see him relaxed on the sofa—instead, the fire was little more than a flicker and the room was empty.

Puzzled, she was about to leave the room when a glimmer of light caught her attention. She moved closer to the bay window and hugged herself against the draft coming off the glass. *What is that?* She leaned forward, squinting through the swirling snow into the pitch-black night. There. There it was again. It almost looked like...

A fire.

Her heart catapulted into her throat as her brain caught up to her eyes. Horror stories of vast tracts of forest going up in smoke fueled her fear. What could she do? The phone. *Hurry, hurry, call for help.* She scrambled to the handset thrown carelessly onto the sofa and dialed the emergency number, her fingers trembling with nerves.

"Come on, come on," she chanted under her breath, but no amount of wishing could get the phone to connect. The storm must be playing havoc with the lines. Another glance out the window showed the lick of flames climbing up the outer wall of the garage Mac had pointed out earlier.

Mac. He must have spotted the blaze, as she had, and rushed outside to put out the fire. He would need help. Giving up on getting through, Sam dropped the phone and raced for the kitchen. She'd noticed a fire extinguisher in the pantry while searching for Cleo's food. Yes, there it was, tucked into a corner and hooked to the wall. She wasted precious seconds figuring out how to undo the clasp before hefting the surprisingly heavy canister into her arms and racing for the door.

A noxious stench of gas and rubber permeated the air. Thick black plumes of smoke drifted above the dark outline of the trees, obscene against the virgin white of the snow.

"Mac," Sam yelled, shocked by the strength of the fire. The heat slapped her chilled skin and she realized she'd run out of the house without a jacket. No time to change that now, the sliding doors of the garage were totally engulfed, and the hungry flames were eating their way to the only other exit—the side door. She had to do something.

She pointed the canister at the door and pulled the trigger. Nothing happened. Vibrating, she looked at the stupid canister. Why had she never taken the time to learn how to use these blasted things? Just as she was about to fling it across the yard, she noticed a ring sticking sideways from the top of the handle. She jerked the pin out and aimed again, and this time a thin spray of foam exploded from the rubber hose. The fire hissed, angry at the creature seeking to destroy its fun. But it knew it would loose against this foe, and baring orange-red fangs, leaped to the roof in a bright burst of sparks.

Relieved, Sam yanked the door open, wincing when the knob burned her palm, and stepped inside. She covered her mouth against the smoke sneaking in through the cracks and gazed nervously around the packed room. The dark outline of a truck ghosted out of the gloom. Hoping against hope, Sam edged her way between ATV's and skidoos, keeping low to avoid the haze creeping down from the ceiling. "Mac," she choked. Where was he?

Mac Wanowski was having the best night of his hockey career. Two goals and three assists with a period and a half to go. Everything was going their way. He should be a shoo-in for MVP. The Victoria WarHawks were playing on home turf to a full stadium of rowdy fans with fast ice—nothing could stop him now.

The blow came out of nowhere.

One minute he was flying down the ice with the puck held in the sweet spot of his stick, the crowd roaring his name, the net in sight, in the next instant Mac was shoved from behind and smacked into the boards. He bounced and went down hard on his right knee. The pain was immediate and intense. It sucked the breath from his lungs and left him seeing stars. He dropped his head between his arms and tried to remain conscious until the medics arrived. It was small consolation the refs caught the illegal move and rang the penalty buzzer.

Fricking Murtagh.

The other team's enforcer liked to pull sneak attacks. He'd done it before. Mac rolled onto his back and blinked as the auditorium swam before his eyes.

"Wow, man, that had to hurt." Samson chortled, skidding to a stop against the boards. The plexi-glass shook with the collision.

Edwards, the team's doctor skated across the ice in his dress shoes and dropped to his side. "Hey, Hammer, nice hit. How you doing?"

"Been better," Mac grumbled. He squinted through the face-shield and yanked off his gloves. "It's the knee, Doc. Screwed it good this time." The helmet came next, clattering onto the ice along with his dreams.

"Don't worry. He will pay." Lazlo, the grinder, towered over Mac glaring at the other team as though daring them to come near.

"Keep it clean, boys," the ref said, gliding up to pat the Croatian's arm. "I don't wanna send you to the bench, but I will." He exchanged a look with the doc, then blew his whistle and waved an arm over his head. "Gurney's on the way."

Mac growled and tried to sit up, but Edwards

forced him down. The guy might be old but working around a bunch of hockey players kept him in shape. "Take it easy, Mac. It's just a precaution. You don't want to aggravate that tendon any more than you need to."

Getting hauled off the ice like an invalid only added insult to injury. Not even the crowd's support could ease his wrath against the meathead who'd taken him down. He strained to see past the EMT's hold on the gurney. Murtagh sat in the penalty box, his arrogant gaze triumphant even as his coach tore him a new asshole from over his shoulder.

Pissed, Mac pointed and mouthed, "You're mine." Then they were in the hallway heading toward the dressing room and his adrenaline waned, leaving him drawn and listless. The knee throbbed, pressing uncomfortably against his protective padding. His shoulder ached from smashing into the wall and his insides jiggled like a bowl full of jelly. But if Doc gave him the go-ahead he could still make the third period. He needed to get out there and support his team, dammit.

Coach was waiting when he arrived, pacing and muttering while running a hand over his thinning pate. The second the EMTs set him down on the exam table Coach was breathing in his face.

"What the hell, Wanowski? I told you to pass! This

superhero complex of yours is costing the team. Now what are we supposed to do, huh? We're already two men down and play-offs are coming up. Your actions tonight might have cost us the season. How do you feel now, asshole?"

Like shit, thanks for asking. The man had it in for him ever since Mac hooked up with his daughter for one never-to-be-repeated night, and nothing he did for the team was enough. It bothered him that this time Coach was right—he'd screwed up. Not that he could admit it, especially with all the interested ears wagging in the room. So, he said nothing.

The coach threw up his hands and stormed out of the room, heading back to what was left of the game. Mac just hoped they could retain their five-three lead until it ended.

"You like playing with fire, don't ya?" Doc Edwards shook his head. "Your contract is almost up with the WarHawks, Mac. Have you given any thought to what comes next?"

Mac frowned at the doc's back as he turned away to open his medical bag. "You hear something you want to tell me about?" He'd given three of his best years to this team. If the franchise planned to trade him off, the least they could do was tell him to his face.

Doc held up his hand. "Don't get your shorts in a

knot, kid. I merely meant you can't play hockey forever. You must have a backup plan, right?'

Kid. Mac grunted as the other man loosened the ties on his knee guard. The resulting relief was quickly replaced by agony as blood rushed to the injury. He clenched his fists against the cool metal of the exam table and stared at the ceiling with its ugly track lighting while Doc poked and prodded the area like a sadist.

No, he didn't have a backup plan—this was it for him. Hockey was in his blood. It fed his dark soul and gave him the only true joy he'd ever known.

He couldn't leave the game.

"How bad, Doc?" He tipped his head to look down the length of his body and swore. Just as he'd thought, the knee was swollen and already showing signs of bruising. Last time he'd injured it, he'd ended up with water under the kneecap and had to have it drained. Fun times.

Edwards snapped an ice pack into action and set it against his skin before meeting his worried gaze. "I won't know for sure until we do x-rays. My best guess is your ACL." Mac winced. "Hopefully it's a sprain instead of a full tear which would mean surgery and months of rehab."

Christ, just what he didn't need right now. He laid

down and covered his eyes with his forearm. "And if it's a sprain?"

"Sorry, Mac. You're still looking at two-to-four weeks recovery time, physio, and preferably crutches. I know someone, Sam Walters, who's good at this sort of injury. I'll call and see what I can get lined up."

Mac let him drone on with his voice of doom, meanwhile inside his stomach twisted into their own disastrous knots.

What was he going to do now?

2

Sᴀᴍ ᴘᴜsʜᴇᴅ her prescription sunglasses onto her nose and squinted against the blinding white of the snow. It was one of those picture postcard days; you know, the type where the beautiful couple are caught kissing in front of the adorable snowman they've just built. He's holding her like he doesn't plan to let go, and she's laughing, head thrown back to show off long, blond locks. Except, in Sam's case her hair leaned more toward strawberry-blond, and the only beautiful person nearby was the famous NHL hockey player she was about to meet—and he wasn't her type.

Mac Wanowski. The Victoria Warhawks not-so-secret weapon. The Hammer, as sports reporters loved to label him, had brought a floundering team to the playoffs two straight years in a row and they were looking good in the standings this season, too. Her uncle, the team's physician, had stressed the importance of getting Wanowski back to work as soon as possible. Like yesterday.

She looked up at the grim-faced warrior who waited impatiently on the front porch of a cabin set into a tall stand evergreens, their tips reaching up to touch the cornflower blue sky. He leaned on a set of crutches, a baggy pair of sports shorts doing nothing to hide the man's masculinity. An unwelcome shiver of awareness fox-trotted up her spine. He was every bit as handsome as the internet depicted him. Not that she was a stalker, or anything. It was research. She needed to know what she was facing.

Trouble. With a capital T.

"I expected something... bigger," she murmured, dismayed. The mountain cabin was modest at best. She was supposed to spend two weeks here? There must be a mistake. She turned accusing eyes on her uncle, but he was already climbing out from behind the driver's wheel to stretch.

"Nice place," she heard him call. "No wonder you keep it a secret." He leaned down to see what was keeping her. "Coming?"

Did she have a choice?

Sighing, Sam climbed out of the old sedan her uncle refused to trade in and joined him at the trunk. She hefted the heavier case before he could, leaving him the overnight bag. "Are you sure this is a good idea?"

He looked perplexed, but she also caught a mischievous twinkle in his eye. "Of course. Mac needs help and you need a job; win-win."

"Uncle Thomas, you better not be trying to set me up. I already told you, I'm happy on my own." Sam slammed the lid harder than she meant to and gave her sole remaining family member a stern look. "Just because you and Aunt June had so many happy years together doesn't mean it's in the cards for me."

His expression turned somber and Sam cursed her unthinking comment. "Your aunt was the best thing that ever happened to this old coot. I miss her every single minute of the day." He grasped her hand where it rested on the trunk. "Mac's one of the good ones, honey, *but* that's not the reason I brought you out here. His career is on the line and I happen to believe in your ability to get him on his skates before the play-offs. Can you do that?"

Could she?

The ultrasound had shown the injury to be moderate, but one glance at the *patient* convinced Sam this wouldn't be a cakewalk. For one thing, he wasn't even supposed to be walking around yet, even if he was on crutches. And didn't the man realize it was winter? Why was he standing there in shorts and no jacket?

She didn't plan on playing nursemaid to a spoiled rich boy, it wasn't in her contract. But it was also obvious the hockey player meant something to her uncle, so she would try her best. For him.

"Yeah," she said, narrowed gaze on her quarry. "I can do it."

Mac stared at the pint-sized female lugging a suitcase that looked as if it weighed as much as she did, and his blood boiled. Never mind he had no idea who she was or why she thought she was staying in his home, he'd been taught to be a gentleman and not being able to help was galling.

Edwards stumbled along behind, his face pale and tired-looking. Mac was worried about his old friend. He'd tried to get the doc to go to a doc but that had gone over like a lead balloon.

"I don't need some quack telling me what's wrong," he'd growled. "I've taken care of you, haven't I? It's just a bug. It'll be gone soon enough."

Wasn't much Mac could say to that and he'd been sidetracked by his own injury, but it had been two weeks—shouldn't he be looking better by now?

"Doc." He greeted the other man while eyeing the

blonde struggling up the stairs with her case. Shit, he hated this. "I see you brought company."

Edwards ascended the steps, his hand reaching out to grasp the woman's elbow to help her balance. The contrast was stark; the middle-aged man with a bald spot on his head and a bit of a paunch, and the willowy woman with vivid blue eyes and a flawless complexion. What was she to the doc? Mac frowned. Why should it matter to him? If the doc wanted a fling and the woman was willing... all the best to them.

The couple finally made it up his stairs and stopped in front of him.

Edwards stretched his hand out to take Mac's in a firm shake. "Mac, you're looking good. Must be all this fresh mountain air, huh?" He grinned, over jovial.

Mac went on the alert. "What's going on, Doc? You heard from the board? I've called the coach a dozen times and get nothing but the runaround. *We'll see*," he muttered. "*It will depend on what your therapist has to say.* I'm going crazy up here."

Edwards nodded, his eyebrows bunching across his lined forehead. "I warned you to stay low. You're an integral part of the team, but no one likes a pain in the ass and that goes double for the coach. You need to back down and let us do our job, so you can do yours. You hear me, Mac?"

Mac squeezed the grips on his crutches while the

red tide of frustration washed through him, leaving him tired and disheartened. "Yeah, I hear you," he said. "When's the therapist arriving? I thought he was coming with you?"

Doc glanced at the woman beside him and something about the stunned look she gave him warned Mac before the words confirmed it. He was already shaking his head when she spoke.

"Not a he, Mr. Wanowski, she. I'm Samantha Walters, your new physiotherapist. You can call me Sam."

Well, shit.

3

THE DISMAY on the hockey player's chiseled face would have been comical if this job didn't mean so much to Sam. Her foothold in a male-dominated industry was tenuous at best. She'd clawed her way through uni and several months of training before building enough of a name to open her own business. A big step, and one she hoped wasn't a mistake.

"Not what you expected?" she asked. Might as well start out as she meant to go on—diplomacy wasn't part of her nature. Just ask her mother.

Wanowski glared at Sam and her uncle. "I don't need a babysitter, Doc. How is *she* going to help me?"

Sam had a few ideas, but he probably didn't want to hear them. "Are you a chauvinist, Mr. Wanowski?"

"Samantha, you're not helping," her uncle chided. He looked small and frail next to the Hulk. "I'm sorry for misleading you, Mac. I should have clarified my niece prefers to go by the name Sam, but trust me, she knows her job. Just give her a chance."

The last thing her uncle needed was stress. If Mr. Negativity thought she would be more hindrance than help, so be it.

Her suitcase thunked onto the wooden deck, a loud punctuation mark in the sudden silence. "Look, if you don't want me here, suit yourself. I have better things to do than to spend my days arguing with a Neanderthal. It's your life, Mr. Wanowski, do with it what you will. I only ask that you allow us a short rest in your home and then we'll be on our way." She lifted her chin, prepared to shove past his brawny chest if it meant getting her uncle inside. It was times like this she wished she'd learned how to drive.

Mac sized her up as though it was her fault he'd been benched, before turning a slightly warmer gaze on Uncle Thomas. "Must have been a *long* drive." He shot the puck in her direction. "I just made a fresh pot of coffee. You may as well come on in. I need to get off my feet anyway. Doctor's orders."

"You obey a command? That must be one for the record books." Sam couldn't resist, the verbal sparring warming her up faster than her down parka.

He frowned, his jaw ticking with annoyance. "You don't know me, Miss Walters, but apparently you have an issue with me. All the more reason our relationship wouldn't work. I need someone who can set their personal prejudices aside long enough to do their job."

Aaand, he scores.

"You two sound like an old married couple," Uncle Thomas muttered.

That froze the bickering better than anything she could come up with. Wanowski opened his cabin door and waved them through. "It's getting cold. There's a storm in the works, you'll want to head out soon."

He must be a blast at the after-parties. Sam stepped around her luggage and waited for her uncle to enter the lion's den. She drew even with the hockey player and hesitated, the force of his presence both intimidating and compelling. "Don't blame him," she said. "He cares about the team and was under the mistaken impression you did too."

Mac grasped her wrist as she went to walk past. "The WarHawks mean everything to me. My problem is you, *Samantha*." He said her name like it was an insult. "I don't like being made a fool of, that's something you might want to remember." He cast her arm aside and entered the house, leaving her shivering on the porch.

The guy was *intense*. The pay wasn't worth it. If she pulled some weekends at the hospital, ate macaroni and cheese, and groveled to her old boss at the diner she might—might—scrape enough together so that she wouldn't lose her office space. For this month anyway.

The cabin came as a surprise. She'd expected dark wood and slate floors to match their host's sable hair, steely-gray eyes and moody demeanor. Instead, the entry was light and airy with a tall ceiling and dormer windows. The walls were painted a sage-green. Hardwood flooring and an iron and glass staircase leading to the second floor completed the modern décor. No moose head wall mounts for this mountain getaway, in its place a stunning abstract caught the light and refracted it back in an array of warm, relaxing tones. It all served to increase her curiosity about Mac, The Hammer, Wanowski. What was his story? Why was he up here, all alone, instead of in the city enjoying the tender loving care of some puck bunny? Her uncle had made it clear Mac was single and a 'stand-up guy', whatever that meant. As far as she was concerned, if he paid her the agreed upon salary and kept his hands to himself, that's all she was interested in. Or should she say, had been interested in—until he'd fired her before she'd even started.

The low murmur of male voices guided her into a cozy den. She had a fleeting impression of walls lined with books, a sleek desk edged in chrome, and a crackling fire behind a steel grate before focusing on her uncle sitting on a leather ottoman inspecting Wanows-ki's knee.

The big man stood with his back to her, impatience radiating from broad shoulders. "It's fine, Thomas. I've been following the R.I.C.E. formula you recommended. Rest, ice, compression," he tapped the elastic bandage circling above and below the joint, "and elevation." He set the crutches aside and sank, with a sigh, onto the matching sofa. His hooded gaze trailed up and down her body before returning to her face. "So, you really think you can fix me before the play-offs?"

Sam bit off a smile. It would take a *lot* longer than two weeks to change this man's attitude. "Yes, I can get you on your feet. I *can't* guarantee you'll be fit to skate. That's going to depend on you."

His hand went to his knee, covering the injury as though he could make it disappear. "I need to get back to my team." He lasered her with his gaze. "Two weeks, Miss Walters. You're hired."

The rush of success racing through Sam's bloodstream was tempered by the six-foot-whatever glaring at her like the possible ruination of his career was her fault.

Let the games begin.

[4]

Mac remained on the sofa brooding while Samantha
—he refused to think of her with a masculine name—
said goodbye to her uncle and no doubt received advice
on how to treat his well-known surly temper.

It hadn't always been that way. His wife's death
changed everything.

"Ready to start?"

Mac jerked, drawn out of the dark pit of memories.
He frowned at the young blonde standing in the doorway. "Start what?" She'd better not expect him to run
laps or some shit.

She tapped her toes in those ridiculous high-heeled
boots she'd worn. "I thought we'd take a walk. See how
that knee is doing under repetitive movement. You up
for it? I totally understand if it's too much for you."

Too much for The Hammer? That'll be the day.

Mac rose, ignoring the ache in his leg to reach for the crutches. "Lead on, Doc." There was no way he was going to admit how bad it hurt. The operating table was the only other option besides therapy, and he didn't plan on going down that road anytime soon.

Fricking Murtagh.

Samantha eyed his bare legs. "I can wait if you want to get some pants on," she muttered, her cheeks turning a becoming pink.

Mac grinned. "Never seen hairy legs before, Doc?" Other than a loose pair of sweats, shorts were the only comfortable clothing he had to fit over his knee.

She shrugged and turned away. "It's your funeral," she said, trouncing down the hall to the front door.

Mac followed, his steps slow and measured. The last thing he needed was to slip and set his recovery back.

Samantha watched him, arms folded under her more-than-a-handful breasts—not that he was noticing.

"Maybe this isn't a good idea," she said, her brows furrowed.

Sweat broke out on his forehead and frustration got the best of him. "Just do your job, Doc. I'll worry about the rest."

She stiffened, her arms dropping to reveal clenched fists. "Anyone ever tell you you're not very nice?"

He chuckled. "You're kidding, right?" He couldn't

say *nice* was something he'd ever been accused of before. Or at least... not in a very long while.

Samantha opened the door and a rush of cold air sent prickles up his legs. Good. It reminded him, not that he needed it, of what was at stake. He grabbed his jacket off the hook and mentally girded himself for the long road ahead.

───────

SAM JERKED AWAKE, gasping. Her heart beat an urgent fight or flight warning, hands clenching the down duvet into a hard ball around her neck. She lay there for a moment, trying to hear over her own raspy breathing. Nothing. The house was silent except for that silly cuckoo clock ticking off the endless minutes of the night.

She never slept well in strange places anyway, and today had been particularly stressful. Mac, The Hammer, Wanowski wasn't making her job easy. He'd made it more than clear what he thought of therapists. Too bad he didn't have a choice; the team managers called the shots—whether he liked it or not.

There it was again.

An eerie moan accompanied by a scratch, scratch, bam. Scratch, scratch, bam.

If Wanowski thought he was going to get rid of her

that easily, he better think again. Sam rolled out of bed and grabbed the first defensive thing she could find, the hardcover book she'd borrowed from the den earlier.

The door creaked like an old woman's knees, instantly ending any element of surprise she might have had. The hall was dark. Quiet. Too quiet.

"Hel... hello?" she asked, her voice little more than a squeak. The book remained clenched over her head, ready for... who knows what. She wished she hadn't skipped those self-defense classes her best friend, Grace, had taken.

Mo-o-o-an.

The hair stood up and tried to run off her neck. Why hadn't she just stayed in her warm, cozy bed hiding under the pillows like any other scaredy-cat would do?

Sam swallowed hard and stepped into the hall. "No... not funny, Mac." She squinted owlishly as a set of glowing green eyes, *halfway up the wall*, turned her way. Sam screamed.

"What the hell?" Mac hollered from his room upstairs.

Not Mac then.

The clunk of crutches on hard wood floors heralded her host's arrival. The lights flicked on and Sam got a blurry eyeful of rumpled, annoyed man glaring at her from the head of the staircase. *Boxers never looked so good.* The random thought warmed her cheeks.

"Do you make a habit of freaking out in the middle of the night, Doc? Because, I gotta tell you, it sucks."

Embarrassed, she dropped the weapon/book to her side, noticed his narrowed gaze on her chest, and brought it up again. Right, her nightshirt was soft and comfortable, but white, and threadbare in spots.

Sam pointed down the hall. "Something was staring at me out of the wall," she accused as though it was his fault.

"Oo-kay." He looked at her like she was crazy before slowly, carefully making his way down the stairs on that bum knee. She'd feel bad if she didn't have the impression he was mocking her.

Mac stopped by the elegant sofa table cleared of everything except a silver filigree picture frame. He straightened it on the table, his fingers almost caressing.

"Who is that?" Sam asked, desperate to disperse the lingering ghosts. She remembered seeing a younger, softer version of Wanowski with a beautiful woman smiling into his eyes. His wife, maybe? Where was she then?

Mac ignored her to bend at the waist, his broad back gleaming under the brass and glass ceiling light. When he rose, a big, black cat rested over one muscular forearm. "I think I found your ghost," he murmured.

Sam smiled. "He's gorgeous. Yours?" She moved hesitantly toward them. "Is he friendly?" She'd been bitten by a neighbor's cat as a child and had never quite recovered from the experience.

Mac nodded, fondling the dark, silky-looking ears. "It's a she. Cleo. And yes, she's a pussycat."

Sam giggled. The man was attractive when he wasn't being a jerk. "When I heard those bumps in the night, I wasn't expecting a harmless feline. Or a badass hockey player to come to my rescue."

His lips tilted in an almost smile. "How do you know the cat is harmless?"

Sam shrugged, her own lips flirting with a smile. She noticed he didn't argue with *his* description. Badass, indeed. This was going to be an interesting two weeks.

5

THE NEXT MORNING Mac woke stiff, sore, and surprisingly refreshed. The doc was right, it was time to kick up his rehabilitation program. Cleo jumped down from her perch on the dresser and gave him the stink eye before slipping out the door like a dark shadow. No wonder she'd scared Samantha last night, she spooked him out with those all-seeing green eyes.

He still remembered the day Jess brought the bedraggled stray home. The kitten had been found in a cardboard box, malnourished and filthy. The animal shelter where she worked was already overcrowded. Jess couldn't allow them to put the poor animal down, so she brought it home—to their condo filled with European leather furniture, silk curtains, and a strict regulation of no pets. Jess had held the kitten up for his inspection, her blue eyes filled with love and laughter and he'd caved like a besotted idiot. She could have brought home a slobbering St Bernard and he would've found a way to make her happy. After her death, he didn't have the heart to give Cleo away, so here they were, three years later and still working on their trust issues.

The loft of the cabin he'd rented from his team-mate, Roy Donaldson, looked out over the eastern slopes of the Vancouver Island mountain ranges, affording him an unparalleled view of stunning blue skies and snow-topped peaks. Hard to imagine he could be skiing all day and sailing the next. The hills were pristine. Too bad he was injured. He loved hitting the slopes now and then. Nothing like racing across crisp, freshly fallen snow with the scent of pine in the air and frost biting his ears. It gave his life clarity outside of a hockey rink. Between off-season practices and the hectic game schedule, sometimes it seemed he lived and breathed hockey. Not that there was anything wrong with that, the sport had been good to him. Saved him really, after Jess.

A door closed downstairs and he was reminded of his unwanted guest. Samantha Walters. She was a contradiction with her shapely body and innocent blue eyes hiding a will of steel. She wasn't afraid of him even though half of the NHL gave him a wide berth. He'd seen through her little ruse to get him walking.

She'd read him like an open book, realizing he wasn't the type of guy to turn away from a challenge. What else had she figured out about him? This was the reason he didn't do shrinks—his thoughts were his own, dammit. And yes, he did realize she wasn't a head doctor, but she might as well be. She'd been playing mind games with him since her arrival.

Well, the sooner he mended, the faster she could leave. With that in mind, he forced his knee through a series of extensions and then squats—which hurt like hell—before rewarding his efforts with a long, hot shower. By the time he dressed and made his way down the stairs, the scent of bacon and pancakes drifted from the kitchen. She cooked. He wasn't sure why that warmed his chest, but it did.

Her back was to him as she stood at the stove, a heaping plate of flapjacks on the counter next to her mug of steaming coffee.

"Looks like you made enough for an army," he said by way of greeting.

She jumped and yelped. The pancake she'd been flipping soared through the air to land on the edge of the two-seater pedestal table before slowly losing its war with gravity to splat on the tile floor—right next to a startled cat. Cleo let out a yowl fit to raise the roof, jumped backward on stiff legs and hissed at the strange oval steaming on the floor.

Mac grinned, not sure which female looked more outraged. "I don't think Cleo is going to give you a stellar review."

Samantha glared at him through a pair of oval cats-eye glasses. "Do you make a habit of sneaking up on people?"

Mac clumped to the coffee machine, snapped a pod into place, and leaned nonchalantly against the counter to wait for his brew. "I thought the crutches would have announced my arrival." He reached for a strip of bacon and frowned when she tapped his fingers with the spatula. "You plan on eating all that by yourself?"

"Maybe," she muttered, covering a yawn with her hand.

Butterflies fluttered in Mac's stomach. He rubbed the spot. The tantalizing aromas must have made him hungrier than he thought. He took a sip of his coffee, then set the cup aside to nudge the doc away from the stove. "I'll finish up. Go sit down and I'll bring it over."

She stared up at him with dazed, sleepy blue eyes that made him feel ridiculously protective. He cleared his throat and waved her away. "Go. It's the least I can do."

She shrugged and handed him the spatula. "Don't burn it, then." She crouched to scrape the pancake off the floor and broke a piece for the cat. "Here, kitty. I'll share with *you*."

Mac suppressed a smile. She was just as feisty as Cleo.

He finished cooking the last of the pancake batter and shut off the stove before hobbling over to the table with the plates perched precariously in his hands.

Samantha watched him, eyes intent on his battered knee. "Is it very painful?"

His first reaction was to deny it, but something made him admit the truth. "Yeah, but that's okay, as long as it heals."

Her gaze became sympathetic and he turned away for the syrup. He didn't need compassion, he needed her to push him past his comfort zone. "What's on today's agenda, Doc?"

She rose to grab the dinner plates and their coffee cups, waiting until they'd loaded up the dishes to answer. "It's Sam, and I thought we'd give snowshoeing a try."

Surprised, he halted the overloaded forkful of food. "Is that safe?" Well, he'd wanted a challenge. He needed to be careful what he wished for.

She nodded. "We won't go far. Besides," she glanced above her head, "you've already been warming up."

He looked up as well, and realized his room was

over the kitchen. She must have heard him exercising earlier. Busted.

"Look, play-offs are coming up soon and I need to be there for my team. I owe them." He took a bite of pancake dripping with syrup to prove his point, but it tasted like sawdust.

Sam tipped her head as though trying to figure him out. "Why do you say that?"

He shrugged, not ready to tell this virtual stranger his life story, even if it did feel as though he'd always known her. "It's greed. I want my name on the Stanley Cup, that's all." He ignored the disappointment on her face to shovel more food into his mouth.

Sam sipped her coffee and glanced surreptitiously at the man sitting across from her. Rather than classically handsome, Mac's face was a combination of rough edges and interesting planes. A broad, intelligent forehead, thick, expressive brows, gray-blue eyes that shifted from mercury to steel in an instant, chiseled cheekbones over a jaw covered with a five o-clock shadow, and lips that set her pulse pounding. His golden-brown hair was surprisingly thick for a guy who wore a helmet to work every day. Parted on the side, it lay ruthlessly over his scalp in an obviously high-end cut, but even that couldn't control the wave over his brow or the one caressing his nape.

"Do I have syrup on my chin?"

Sam's gaze flew to his amused one. "Huh? No. I was just... thinking, that's all."

"Okay. Penny for them?" he teased.

She attempted to laugh it off, but it fell flat. "Do you ever wish you could change one thing from your past?" Where had that come from? Mac didn't care about her mistakes. He was a client, no more, no less. She'd better keep that in mind. "Never mind. I shouldn't have asked."

He shook his head. "No, that's a fair question. I think we all have something we wish we could change. I was married once." He smiled faintly, lost in memories. "She was my girlfriend in high school. We were together for eight years before she...." He pushed away from the table. "We should go. It gets dark early here."

Sam nodded and watched pensively as he hobbled out of the room on his crutches. Obviously, they'd been deeply in love.

While Cleo lapped milk from a bowl in the corner, she rose and began to clean their breakfast dishes, aware she'd lost a chance to come clean about why she was really there.

6

THE AIR WAS CRISP, the sky a clear robin's egg blue, and the view wasn't bad either. Mac grinned as Sam bent over to tighten her snowshoes, her heart-shaped ass mouthwatering in a pair of Pepto pink tights that matched her down ski jacket topped off with a white fur-lined knitted hat. She could have modeled for a sports magazine in that getup and had thousands of guys drooling over her. It made him wonder why she'd chosen to become a therapist.

"Are you staring at me?" she asked, catching him off guard.

He shrugged and stomped his feet to check his own bindings. "I was just wondering what made you take up therapy in school. It's basically a thankless job, isn't it? Dealing with a bunch of angry, frustrated clients doesn't sound like a ball of laughs to me."

She tucked a few stray strands of honey-blond hair under her hat before meeting his eyes, her gaze intense. "Is that what you are, Mac? It's okay to be discouraged, you know. Getting injured is scary, your body doesn't feel like your own. But I *will* get you on the road to recovery, trust me."

The only person Mac fully trusted was dead.

He anchored the crutches under his arms and started across the field toward the frozen lake in the distance. It didn't take long to get into a semi-comfortable rhythm and he let the past go to enjoy the moment. A quick glance over his shoulder showed Sam following close behind with rosy cheeks and sparkling eyes to rival the winter skies.

"You've done this before," he accused. What else did she have up her sleeve?

She smirked. "My parents took us to Tahoe every Christmas until I turned fourteen."

He leaned on his crutch and unobtrusively eased weight off his knee. "What happened then?" Was the pain less today? It seemed like it might be getting...

"My dad died."

The words dropped like a bomb. The shock reverberated through Mac's chest, shards of ice decimating his heart. It was as though he'd returned to the nightmare days of his own loss. The anger and despair, the deep, dark pit of desolation he'd embraced as penance for not protecting Jess—he should have kept her safe.

"How?" The words were little more than a husky rattle, but he was powerless to hide behind his tough guy image right now. He could see it in her eyes, she was one, too. A reluctant survivor.

She hugged herself and stared at the windswept ice of the lake peeking through the virginal snow. "A heart attack. He'd been out skiing with Kevin all day, came home and collapsed." She sniffled and tugged off her gloves to wipe at her eyes. "Just like that, he was gone. I always wondered if there was something we missed, you know? A sign of what was wrong, that he needed help."

He told himself empathy drew him to her side. He had no excuse for cupping her cheek. No explanation for the jolt of electricity that made his fingers tingle and pulse throb. Her beautiful blue eyes darkened behind tortoiseshell lenses, the awareness palpable between them. Mac shifted closer, intent on tasting those pretty pink lips until he stepped down wrong and his knee twisted painfully under his weight.

"Dammit," he growled, dropping his crutches so he could clutch the aching joint.

"Mac, what happened? Are you all right?" Her hand fluttered over his shoulder before she plopped down in the snow to get a better look. "Let me see," she ordered, gently, but firmly, slipping under his grip to check the torn ligament.

He stared at her bent head, cursing himself for a fool. What was he doing, allowing a passing attraction to jeopardize his career? He needed to focus on recovery. No more distractions.

He took a careful step back, breaking contact. "It's fine, Doc. I'll ice it later. Let's finish this damn walk, already."

Sam stared up at him, her gaze turbulent, before rising with his crutches in hand. She swept the clinging snow from the hand grips and passed them over. "Sure. I'm ready when you are."

"Fine," he snapped, angry as much with himself as with her easy dismissal. He turned and started the return trip, taking a shortcut through the trees where the snow wasn't as deep.

"What's your problem, Wanowski?"

Sam's breathless shout drew him up short. He turned, surprised, and suffering a pang of guilt by the distance between them. "I thought you said you could keep up." Better to retain the aggression between them. Safer.

She puffed out a disgusted laugh. "I didn't know you planned a marathon."

He grinned, watching as she picked her way toward him. Damn, but he liked her sense of humor.

She didn't take any flack, either. If he was being honest with himself—something he tended to avoid these days —he'd have to admit he hadn't been fair to Sam. He'd acted like an ass from the moment they'd met. He was lucky she hadn't packed up and returned to the city with her uncle. The real issue was she was a good-looking woman and he was drawn to her when he didn't want to be attracted to anyone ever again. Sex was one thing, he was a man, after all. He'd slept with his share of hockey babes after... But, none of them mattered. They helped to blow off steam, that's all.

Sam was... different.

"Hurry up, I'm getting old waiting on you," he called, just to see her eyes flash. He wasn't disap-pointed.

She stooped mid-stride and scooped up a handful of snow encrusted with pine needles and debris. "You know," she mused, "I've been listening to your sarcasm for two long days now." Tossing the ball from hand to hand she eyed him like he was the bullseye at a county fair game of chance.

Mac was fairly certain she wouldn't risk him twisting his knee again while avoiding her retribution, but just in case, he glanced around for a tree large enough to hide his bulk. And that was when he noticed the hunter. The man wore dark camo fatigues and had a black balaclava over his face, though it really wasn't that cold. The high-powered rifle looked like an exten-sion of his arms, the scope big enough there was little doubt he could see what he was aiming for. Which didn't explain why it was pointed their way. Sam was easily identifiable in her cotton candy getup, even if he was in dark leather—stupid choice, now that he thought about it.

He took a step forward and raised his arms to let the guy know they were there. "Hey, don't shoo..." Before he could finish, a loud crack reverberated through the forest, followed by a high-pitched scream.

Sam. He turned toward the spot he'd last seen her just as another crack exploded nearby and something struck him from behind, knocking him to the ground.

7

SAM LAY on the ground at Mac's back, mewling cries of terror crawling up her throat and blocking any possible clues of their assailant's location. Someone was freaking *shooting* at them. Who got up in the morning and decided, *I'm going to shoot someone today.* Couldn't he tell they weren't deer or moose or whatever *the hell* he was aiming at?

Shaking, she ran trembling fingers over Mac's torso, praying like she'd never prayed before that he hadn't been hit. "I'm sorry I knocked you over," she sobbed. "Please, M... Mac, talk to me. I'm so sc... scared."

"Shh," he snarled, throwing a hard glance over his shoulder. His gaze narrowed. "Are you hit?"

Shocked into silence, she dabbed her brow and lowered her hand to stare blankly at the reddish-brown streak staining the threads of her white mitt. "I...." She swallowed hard. "It's a scratch, I'm fine." They had bigger problems at the moment.

He considered her for a moment, then gave a short nod. "Probably some dumbass hunter. We'll stay low for a bit, see if he moves on." He turned his attention to the trees, searching out the monster in their midst.

Sam ducked her head to make a smaller target. Her cheek brushed the sandpaper-like surface of the snow and she inhaled the crushed pine needles under their bodies. Her mind filled with images of her family; Dad teaching them to fly fish, Kevin racing his tricycle to keep up to her and her friends, Mom encouraging her to go after her dreams. She covered her mouth to hold back the sobs. Would she ever see them again?

When she'd seen that gun pointed their way, her heart stopped. One second, she'd been contemplating the best place to hit Mac with her snowball and the next she'd seen that hunter and instinct had taken over. If he'd been shot... well, he wasn't. If they got out of this in one piece, she was calling Uncle Thomas to pick them up. A mountain cabin was no place to be during hunting season—unless your name was Davy Crockett.

"I think he's gone. We should be safe now." Mac rolled onto his back and winced.

Contrite, Sam laid a hand on his broad chest. "Did I hurt you? I'm sorry."

He turned his head to meet her gaze. "Who taught you to tackle like that, an old boyfriend?"

She smiled. "My brother, actually. He went to college on a football scholarship."

"Ahh. Remind me to thank him sometime." He closed his hand over hers and squeezed. "You're quite the woman, Samantha Walters."

Sam melted under the warmth of his regard. "Maybe you can meet him after we get off this mountain."

He stiffened. "I'm not going anywhere."

She sat up, oblivious to danger. "Are you nuts? You can't be serious. What if something happens and you're up here all by yourself? Who's going to help you then, you big oaf?" Frustrated, she rose and dusted off her pants, keeping an eye out for any movement in the forest around them.

Maybe because of the gunshots, or maybe it was due to their little squabble, but the cheerful chirping chickadees and raucous squawks of jays had been replaced by an eerie silence. The shadows had lengthened since they'd started out just after lunch, and now stretched long, dark fingers through the broad branches of towering hemlock and fir trees. It all served to reinforce Sam's decision; she was going back to the city where she belonged—with or without Mr. Tough Guy Wanowski.

"Can you get up on your own?" she asked, reaching for the discarded crutches. When she turned back, it was to see Mac, powerful arms braced, balancing his weight on the palms of his hands. In the next instant, he pushed upward, as smooth as a puma's pounce, and landed on his feet with barely a wince.

Show off. Still fuming, Sam tossed him his crutches and clumped toward the cabin, wishing she could ditch the awkward snowshoes and sprint to safety. They walked in silence for about ten paces before Mac had to ruin it.

"Are you always this tempestuous?"

The dulcet tone of his voice scraped on her last nerve. "Aren't you the least concerned? That hunter had a scope, he had to see us." She stomped her foot, sending a puff of snow into the air.

"I know," he said, so quietly she stopped to hear him better. He met her gaze and shrugged. "It's not the first time."

Sam gasped. "Someone shot at you before?"

He shook his head. "God, no, nothing like that." He guided them into a thick stand of trees and put himself between her and the last place they'd seen the stranger. "More like warnings. The first one happened just before Murtagh slammed me against the boards a couple of weeks ago at the Philly game. There was a note in my locker, *stay out of our way.*" He caught her skeptical look and smiled. "Yeah, I thought it was a team prank, too, and would have brushed it off except..."

Sam frowned. "Except what?"

"Some threatening phone calls. I told Coach and he pretty much laughed it off, said I was bound to make a few enemies along the way." He looked down at the thick padding around his knee. "I guess he was right."

Was he suggesting his injury might be connected to the threats he'd already received? The gunshots? Her breathing sawed in and out of her throat in sync with her pounding pulse. The forest wavered, and she realized she was on the edge of a panic attack. A warm male hand cupped the back of her neck and forced her head between her knees.

"Slow down there, Doc. I don't want to pack you out of the woods."

His dubious chivalry made her sputter. "Th... thanks for nothing. Let go, you're choking me."

"Not yet," he mumbled, easing the pressure so she could lift her head to glare at him. "Look, I'm sorry I dragged you into this. I told the coach I could heal myself, but he insisted on physio and Doc Edwards suggested you and here we are; sitting ducks for whatever game these guys are playing."

Sam tugged off her mitt and reached for the cell

phone inside her jacket pocket. "We need to call the police. They'll know what to do."

Mac shook his head. "You're wasting your time. There's little or no cell coverage on the mountain, and even if there was, the cops won't do anything. We have no proof."

She unlocked her phone, and sure enough, no reception. Great. Well, there was a landline at the cabin, she could use that. Once the police were involved, she'd feel much...

"What are you scheming up now?" Mac drew his glove back on and nodded at her to do the same. "Evening's coming, we better get a move on before we become wolf bait to top off an already shitty day."

He had that right. Except, there'd been moments today Sam didn't regret. She stared at Mac's broad back, then pushed off behind him, careful to stay close this time.

———

THE PHONE JANGLED in the cramped coach's office of the Victoria WarHawks. Dan stared at the old-fashioned rotary style instrument and stifled the urge to wing it across the room. He knew who was on the other end and had nothing to say to the prick.

The phone rang again.

Unfortunately, he had no choice. He slapped the handset against his ear. "Harris."

"I thought you told me you had things under control?" The voice on the other end was damn near as irritating as the phone.

He glared at the whiteboard taking up most of the landscape on the far wall. It was marked with red. Filled with plays he'd worked hours to perfect. When had he allowed politics to mess with his love of the sport?

"Who says it ain't?" Dan snapped. His patience for this entire mess was done, and he wanted it over. Maybe it was time to retire, escape the rat race. His chest grew heavy just thinking about quitting. Not yet. He could make this right. He just needed some time.

"The playoffs begin in two weeks, Harris."

No kidding. He stood and paced to the end of the phone cord, tempted to wrap it around his neck. "Everything is going according to plan. We'll be ready."

"You'd better be." The sinister tone was accompanied by a sharp click.

Angered, Dan threw the handset at the wall, then cringed when the cradle hit the floor. He slumped into his creaky desk chair and rested his chin in his cupped hand. Twenty-five years in the business and he'd never done anything like he was being forced to do now. It soured his stomach.

There was a quick rap, and Doc poked his grizzled head around the door. "You throw a party without me?"

Dan sighed and waved him in. "Get in here, you old coot." He waited until his old friend sat on the rickety wooden chair on the other side of his desk before opening a drawer and pulling out a half empty bottle of whiskey and two tumblers.

Thomas raised a bushy eyebrow. "Want to talk about it?"

"Not really." Dan took a bracing swig of his drink, then squeezed his eyes shut against the burn. He opened them to see Doc eyeing him with a worried expression. He waved the concern away. "You leaving me to drink alone? C'mon, celebrate with me. The team's looking good to bring the cup home this year. It's our turn, right?" *Like it was three years ago.* He rubbed his bum knee and took another drink, this one going down with barely a bite.

Doc raised his glass in a toast, took a sedate sip of his whiskey, and set the tumbler on the desk. "If we can get The Hammer ready, we'll be golden."

The Hammer. Wanowski was at the root of Dan's problems. The guy was a freaking bullet on the ice— nothing could touch him. Well, nothing that wasn't planned out anyway. His gaze moved to his play board again. If he was caught, his career was over; he'd already been warned he'd take the fall himself. Ironic, considering he wouldn't even be in this situation without them.

"How's our wonder boy's recovery coming, anyway?" There would be no recovery if their man did his job.

"Good." Doc grinned. "Sam's keeping him on his toes. She's calling me tonight with an update."

Dan froze, his drink halfway to his lips. "Samantha?" His voice came out squeaky. He hoped his friend would put it down to the alcohol. "What the hell is Sam doing out there?" He set the whiskey down before he sent the glass the way of the phone. "Christ, Thomas, what were you thinking?" His chest tightened, panic flaring. His forehead broke out in a cold, pimply sweat. Samantha was his goddaughter, for Pete's sake.

And now she was in the crosshairs of a killer.

Doc leaned forward, his forehead a roadmap of hills and valleys. "She's an accredited therapist, if that's what you're worried about. She's had a tough time lately, I didn't see the harm in giving her an opportunity to prove herself with the organization. Maybe, they'll give her a contract."

Or a bullet.

Dan scrubbed a rough hand over his face. He had

to fix this before she got hurt. If it wasn't already too late. Christ.

"You trust your granddaughter with a hockey player? I thought you had more sense than that." He rose to chase down his phone, put the pieces back together and set it in front of Doc. "Call and tell her we'll drive out and pick her up." He forced a chuckle. "I could use a break before the chaos begins; I'll go with you."

Instead of falling in with his plan, Doc shook his head. "I can't do that, Dan. That girl deserves her chance. I'm not taking it away from her." He pushed the phone aside and used the edge of the desk to help him rise. "I gotta get back to work. Thanks for the drink." He hesitated at the door, rubbed a broad finger over the bridge of his nose, then grasped the door knob. "You've always been there for Samantha. She just wants a chance to pay it back. Don't take it away from her. Please."

He slipped out, leaving Dan staring in frustration at the battered phone. *Great, just freaking great.*

8

MAC HALTED on the edge of the tree line and calculated the distance between them and the relative protection of the cabin. He'd assured Sam their shooter was nothing more than an inept hunter, but he wasn't so sure. Something about the guy's stance and his effort to stay hidden, even after the *accidental* shot, didn't make sense. As soon as they got to the landline he planned to call Doc and get Sam off the mountain.

"Tired?" she asked, her husky voice a warm caress.

He turned and a wry smile twisted his lips. Her perky hat was squashed on one side from her fall, twigs embedded in the thick white fur and one lone jaunty leaf sticking out of the top like Robin Hood's feather.

"What's so funny?" she asked, glancing over her shoulder.

Now the smile became a grin. "You have a... ah..." He plucked the feather/leaf from her cap.

"Oh," she said, startled. She met his gaze with a sparkle lighting her incredible blue eyes. "Don't like my fashion sense?"

He liked that about her. She had a quirky sense of humor. They'd been through a stressful day and here she was, a beautiful smile on those luscious lips as she made fun of her dishevelment. Sam wasn't like any woman he'd ever met. "I like it... you, just fine," he admitted.

She blushed adorably. "You're not so bad yourself." She shivered and stared wistfully at the promising heat of the cabin. "Is it safe?"

Which proved she was as smart as she was gorgeous.

"I guess we'll find out." He readjusted the crutches under his arms. "I'll go first. Wait a few minutes, then follow."

She shook her head and pushed past before he realized what she was up to.

"Sam," he called, trying not to trip over his snowshoes as he got turned around. "Give me skates over these rabbit feet any day," he muttered. "Sam, wait."

"Not sure if you heard, Wanowski, but it's the twenty-first century, women's lib is a thing. Besides. I'm not the one who's injured." She set off at a brisk pace, her snow bunny outfit a bright splash of color in the black and white scenery.

In other circumstances, he might have been tempted to explore the sparks between himself and the therapist, but Mac wasn't looking for a relationship, and she had *serious enquiries only* written all over her delectable body.

The cabin was silent as they approached, a thin strip of smoke from the propane furnace the only sign of life. Well, that and the fresh set of boot prints circling the house and leaving tracks through the skiff of snow on the stairs. He was glad now he'd thought to lock the door on their way out. Donaldson had assured him the neighbors treated each other like family, but he was a city boy—old habits died hard.

"We had a visitor," Sam stated, her gaze apprehensive as she halted to wait for him.

For some reason he made light of it, though his own instincts said it wasn't good. "Probably a neighbor looking for a cup of sugar. Let's get inside and get a fire going, those clouds look like snow."

They removed their snowshoes and stood them up in the snowbank like sentinels at the gate before climbing the stairs. The large boot prints faded near the top where the overhang covered the front deck, then picked up again where the stranger returned to the steps and exited around the side of the house. If not for the incoming storm, Mac would be tempted to drive Sam back to Victoria himself. She'd have to spend the night and then he'd see about getting her out of here.

Not him, though. He'd had plenty of time to think since his injury and he wasn't liking what his gut was telling him. The hunter cemented his fears. If he was right, whoever it was would be back—and he planned to be ready for him.

SAM STOMPED her feet to remove the crusty snow from her borrowed boots and waited for Mac to unlock the door. Lucky for her, she was the same size as whoever stayed here before. She'd been woefully unprepared, and not just for the mountain. Mac was different than she'd expected; intense, focused, protective—intriguing.

He also came with baggage.

The haunting loneliness when he'd gazed at the framed photo in the house was impossible to ignore. It was obvious he cared deeply for the woman in that picture, whether or not they were separated. And why had she jumped to that conclusion anyway?

Because he looks at me like he wants me, that's why.

"I thought you were cold?"

She jumped, startled out of her reverie. Mac stood

beside the open door, his expression more impatient than amorous. *Idiot.* She hurried to the door, but a sudden thought had her skidding to a stop. "What if your... neighbor is inside?"

Instead of making light of her fears, Mac set aside his crutches to grasp her hand. "Not buying my explanation, then?" He held up the leather key fob with the WarHawks distinctive logo. "I locked up before we left. You're safe." He didn't add, *"for now."*

She looked from him to the disappearing footprints, to the darkening sky and squeezed his fingers. "I'm glad."

Mac grinned. "That's my girl." He stared into her eyes. "I won't let anything happen to you."

The way he said it, as though making a vow, sent a shiver up her spine. What was going on here?

"Mac—" She started to demand an explanation, but just then Cleo appeared, making a mad dash for the open door.

"Quick, close the door." He yanked her inside and into his arms, shutting the door on the cat's nose. Cleo meowed her displeasure and slinked down the hall. "She's an escape artist. It's a game we play." He smiled, then stilled. His hands tightened on her waist as his gaze focused on her lips. "We should..."

Yes, we should. Except... "Are you married?" The

words burst from her mouth. She immediately wished them back when his gaze darkened.

He released his grip, stepping awkwardly to the side, then cursed as he put weight on his bad leg. "No," he retorted. "She died three years ago, not that it's any of your business."

She cringed, at the raw pain lancing his voice. "I... I'm sorry."

He brushed her away like a pesky fly. "It doesn't matter. It's over and done." He flicked on the lights, dispersing the shadows in the room, if not the ones in his eyes. "I think we're safe enough for tonight, I'm heading up to bed. Have a good evening, Doc."

Without another glance, he trudged up the stairs and disappeared from view.

"Good night," she whispered, the ache in her chest making it hard to breathe. Cleo wrapped her sinuous body between her legs. Sam reached down, lifted the cat into her arms and buried her face in the silky fur. "I'm in big trouble, kitty cat. I think I'm falling for your master. What am I going to do?" Cleo's only answer was a rumbling purr. At least one of them was content.

9

Mac reached the top of the staircase and hesitated. He should have made sure the house was secure, instead he'd stomped off like a kid denied his favorite toy. It wasn't Sam's fault he was such a screwed-up mess. If only... He turned with the intention of returning downstairs, but the sight of her blond head bent over his ex-wife's pet cat stopped him in his tracks. His chest tightened. Losing Jess had gutted him. He couldn't go there again. He liked Sam. Too much to risk her getting hurt like...

Wait a minute.

Mac fell backward, hard enough to rattle the framed prints hanging on the wall. He barely noticed, his mind filled with the horrible possibility. What if *he* was to blame for his wife's death? It had been the play-offs then, too. The WarHawks led the division two-one and the media were having a field day with it. They were the upstarts; the team voted least likely to succeed. He'd heard rumors of some heavy betting going down, but none of that mattered to him. He was in it to win it. And then the phone call came, informing him his pregnant wife was fighting for her life after a horrifying car accident. The trip from the rink was a blur; the race through emergency a nightmare. Eight hours later, they were gone.

He found out later the police were treating the *incident*, as they called the end of his world, suspicious, and had launched an investigation, but nothing came of it. He'd taken the rest of the season off to get his bearings, then threw himself into practice, desperate to outrun his past. Time had dulled the pain, but he'd never forgiven himself for not being there that day. She'd asked him to drive her to her prenatal appointment and he'd forgotten, too busy running plays to take his own wife to the doctor. He had to live with his mistake. He refused to make another one.

Two sets of eyes, one laser green, the other a quizzical blue watched his descent. For a standoffish feline, Cleo seemed to be making herself at home in Sam's arms. Lucky cat.

"Forget something?" Sam murmured, and why did he think she was thinking illicit thoughts?

He cleared his throat, suddenly perspiring for no

reason. "The door... I forgot to lock it for the night." Sealing himself and an incredibly brave, sexy woman inside.

She rubbed her button nose in Cleo's dark fur before carefully setting her down. "I could have done that. You shouldn't be stressing your knee out on the stairs."

He wasn't an invalid for crying out loud. "It's *fine*. Quit coddling me, Doc." He stomped past and threw the deadbolt on the door. His stomach rumbled, reminding him it had been a while since their pancake breakfast. Resigned to spending a few more hours in her company, Mac gestured toward the kitchen. "I'm going to make some dinner. You hungry?"

Her smile could have lit the hallway. "I thought you'd never ask. Pancakes are about as far as my domestic accomplishments stretch. I usually order in." She glanced through the side window where big white snowflakes drifted gently to the ground. "Something tells me we're out of the delivery zone."

Mac bathed in her exuberance. She was like a breath of fresh air after the frozen wasteland of the last few years. If he wasn't careful, he could find himself hooked on Samantha Walters and that wouldn't be fair to her. He wasn't a good bet.

"Unless you plan on getting a reindeer to transport a meal up here, I'm afraid you're stuck with me."

Smooth, Wanowski. His social graces were sadly lacking, not that he'd cared—before now. "I've been told I make a mean omelette."

"You're obviously a man of many talents," she teased. "Lead on, maestro."

He needed to shore up his defenses first. "See what's in the refrigerator, I'll start a fire in the den."

Cleo yowled from the kitchen doorway. Sam laughed. "She talks to you."

Mac shook his head at the crazy cat. "You mean she orders me around. I'm not sure which one of us is boss. Her food is in the pantry, do you mind?"

Sam moved toward the finicky feline. "Of course not. Come on, Cleo, let's get you fed." She sent him a quick glance and a slightly nervous smile before disappearing into the other room.

He could relate. She made him edgy, too. Probably not in the same way though. Sighing, he hobbled down the hall and into the den, dark except for the mellow sheen coming from the flurry outside the paned window. The snow had picked up in volume, the accompanying breeze turning the field and forest into a winter wonderland. He was concerned with the road leading up to the cabin. If this continued, Sam might not get out. He could drive if he had to, but with his right knee screwed up, it wasn't the safest thing in the world and he wasn't sure of her abilities. Donaldson had mentioned it was rare, but he'd seen sudden squalls on the mountain that virtually covered vehicles and made the road impassible. He hoped this wasn't one of those occasions.

He flicked the switch on the wall; at least the lights still worked. Not so lucky for the phone, though. He set the receiver down and frowned. Maybe the storm was worse further down the hill and had knocked down a phone line, or... It was the *or* that worried him the most.

He stopped long enough to light a match to the kindling he'd prepared earlier in the stone fireplace, added a few larger sticks and clutched the poker as he slipped back down the hall, careful not to disturb Sam with her head in his fridge. She'd fiddled with his portable stereo and was jiggling her hips to Ariana Grande while Cleo sat on his counter—where she wasn't allowed—tail twitching to the beat. Or, more likely, waiting for a juicy morsel to land on the floor. He was shocked by how much he ached to join them; to set his suspicions aside and turn back time to the fun guy he'd been in college. He barely remembered that man. Once he was picked up by the NHL everything went crazy. It was a different, exciting new world and he'd gobbled it up; the comradery, the money, sponsorships, but most of all the wins. He became addicted to the game. And it had cost him his wife.

He continued down the hall and out the front door, opting to hobble rather than fight with the crutches. The snow was accumulating, fat flakes that coated the steps and crept onto the deck in a frothy white wave. Once again, he cursed his knee—fresh powder and he couldn't take advantage of it. Skiing was almost as big an adrenaline rush as hockey. He'd met Jess on Whistler. She'd been pure poetry on the hills, the spoiled daughter of a banker. He'd been captivated. They were married six months later and had eighteen months together before she was killed. Little more than a moment, really.

The air had turned brisk. An intermittent wind sent snow dancing around his head as he made his way around the side of the house. It was dark here, quiet with the forest encroaching on the edge of the property, circling ever closer to taking its land back. Mac wasn't superstitious, but he had a healthy respect for the supernatural, and his instincts were nudging him to get the hell out while he could.

He would have missed it if not for the wind grabbing the wire and throwing it into the air like a gleeful child with a skipping rope. He lunged for the end and stared down at the neat slice. Someone had deliberately cut the phone line. They knew there was no cell reception on the mountain and they were trying to stop them from calling for help.

Urgency drove him through the gathering drifts to the double car garage behind the cabin. Mac's pulse stuttered. The door was ajar.

He tightened his grip on the fireplace poker and edged into the dank room, grimacing as the door squeaked a warning of his arrival. Three narrow panes of glass ran across the top of each garage door and afforded him slivers of light to see by. The closest stall contained an assortment of Donaldson's toys; snow machines, quads, and dirt bikes. No wonder Samson liked to spend time here, he'd made himself a sweet haven.

Mac limped between the machinery, keeping his head low. A shuffling step on the other side of his truck had him freezing in his tracks. This was his chance. If he could catch this guy, maybe he could find out what was going on. He circled the back of the pickup, hoping whoever it was would be too occupied to see him coming. The door to the passenger side was open, the interior light off. Instead, his uninvited guest seemed to be going through the items in his glovebox with a penlight. What the hell?

"Hey," he said, working to keep his voice casual. "Looking for something?"

The stranger stiffened. He backed out of the cab, hands out to the sides. "Take it easy, there. I was just checking things out as a friendly neighbor. Strange truck and all."

Plausible excuse, except he happened to be wearing the same type of camo gear as the guy who'd taken potshots at them earlier.

"Turn around, real easy-like," Mac ordered. "I want to meet my *neighbor* face-to-face." He kept his weapon ready, just in case.

The next few seconds happened in slow motion. The intruder turned and flashed the light right into Mac's eyes at the same time he felt a presence at his back. He started to turn, saw a shovel coming at his head and ducked, but not fast enough to stop it from glancing off his temple. Fireworks exploded in his brain as he fell against the side of the truck.

"Sam," he murmured, just as everything went black.

10

SAM REMOVED a full container of eggs, a tomato, an onion, a bright yellow banana pepper, and a block of cheddar cheese from the refrigerator and used her butt to close the door. She juggled her armload past the cat and dumped it on the granite countertop. "Okay, Cleo, your turn." She stooped to scratch her between the ears, then returned to the fridge. "Does Dad give you milk, hmm?" The carton was in the door, the seal broken, so she gave it a sniff before deigning it good enough for her new four-footed friend. A quick search of the pantry and Cleo the cat was daintily eating her dinner, ears flicking at every little sound.

Sam frowned. How long did it take to start a fire? Maybe Mac was taking his time so she'd do the cooking. Not happening. She wandered down the hall, expecting to see him relaxed on the sofa—instead, the fire was little more than a flicker and the room was empty.

Puzzled, she was about to leave the room when a glimmer of light caught her attention. She moved closer to the bay window and hugged herself against the draft coming off the glass. *What is that?* She leaned forward, squinting through the swirling snow into the pitch-black night. There. There it was again. It almost looked like...

A fire.

Her heart catapulted into her throat as her brain caught up to her eyes. Horror stories of vast tracts of forest going up in smoke fueled her fear. What could she do? The phone. *Hurry, hurry, call for help.* She scrambled to the handset thrown carelessly onto the sofa and dialed the emergency number, her fingers trembling with nerves.

"Come on, come on," she chanted under her breath, but no amount of wishing could get the phone to connect. The storm must be playing havoc with the lines. Another glance out the window showed the lick of flames climbing up the outer wall of the garage Mac had pointed out earlier.

Mac. He must have spotted the blaze, as she had, and rushed outside to put out the fire. He would need help. Giving up on getting through, Sam dropped the phone and raced for the kitchen. She'd noticed a fire extinguisher in the pantry while searching for Cleo's food. Yes, there it was, tucked into a corner and hooked to the wall. She wasted precious seconds figuring out how to undo the clasp before hefting the surprisingly heavy canister into her arms and racing for the door.

A noxious stench of gas and rubber permeated the air. Thick black plumes of smoke drifted above the dark outline of the trees, obscene against the virgin white of the snow.

"Mac," Sam yelled, shocked by the intensity of the fire. The heat slapped her chilled skin and she realized she'd run out of the house without a jacket. No time to change that now, the sliding doors of the garage were totally engulfed, and the hungry flames were eating their way to the only other exit—the side door. She had to do something.

She pointed the canister at the door and pulled the trigger. Nothing happened. Vibrating, she looked at the stupid canister. Why had she never taken the time to learn how to use these blasted things? Just as she was about to fling it across the yard, she noticed a ring sticking sideways from the top of the handle. She jerked the pin out and aimed again, and this time a thin spray of foam exploded from the rubber hose. The fire hissed, angry at the creature seeking to destroy its fun. But it knew it would lose against this foe, and baring orange-red fangs, leaped to the roof in a bright burst of sparks.

Relieved, Sam yanked the door open, wincing when the knob burned her palm, and stepped inside. She covered her nose against the smoke sneaking in through the cracks and gazed nervously around the packed room. The dark outline of a truck ghosted out of the gloom. Hoping against hope, Sam edged her way between ATV's and skidoos, keeping low to avoid the haze creeping down from the ceiling. "Mac," she choked. *Where are you?*

She was about to give up and head back the way she'd come when a moan reached her ears over the crackling laugh of the beast. Her heart a hard ball in her throat, she crept around the rear of the truck and gasped, "Mac."

He lay crumpled against the tire, his body folded like an accordion. He flinched at the sound of her voice and lifted bleary eyes in her direction. "What happened?"

Sam hurried over and crouched at his side. "The garage is on fire. We need to get out of here. Are you hurt?" Her hands fluttered nervously. He seemed disoriented and barely glanced up at the roaring going on overhead. If they didn't move soon, she was scared the roof might fall on their heads. "Can you stand?"

There was no way she could drag him out on her own —he out-weighed her by a hundred pounds.

"Doc," he murmured, his voice slurred. "You're pretty when you're bossing me around."

She sat on her heels, nonplussed. Should she be flattered or insulted that he would compliment her in such a backhanded fashion? And what did he mean by *bossing*? She wasn't a bully. Her training had taught her the necessity for... A shower of sparks hailed down from above and she screamed and covered her head in terror. When she got brave enough to peek out from between her arms it was to see Mac's pants smoldering below the knee. "Aah," she cried, and grabbed the half-empty fire canister. A short spray covered his leg in foam and thankfully extinguished the embers.

Mac stared at her befuddled. "What the hell, over?"

She would smile at his outraged glare, but there wasn't time. "Unless you have a dream of becoming a toasted S'more, we need to get out of here. Now, get up!"

Her panic must have got through to him, he grunted and groaned but managed to leverage himself up, using the truck for balance.

"Where are your crutches?" she asked, searching the nearby floor in the gloom.

He shrugged, then winced, his hand going to the

back of his skull. "I feel like someone hit me with a sledgehammer."

Lovely. No supports and a half-conscious hockey player to remove from the jaws of hell. A day at the park.

"Hang on to me." Sam tucked herself under the arm braced on the truck and encouraged him to walk. "One step at a time. You can do this."

It was slow going, and more of a shuffle than a step, but they made it to the ATVs before needing a break. Both were gasping by then, the air hot and toxic around them.

Mac leaned hard on the seat of the quad, his shoulders bunched in agony. "Go without me," he muttered. "I'm going to get you killed."

Sam ignored him. Scared as she was, there was no way she'd leave without him. "Only about ten more feet and we're clear. Come on, Wanowski, show me what you're made of."

He flashed her a smile from his soot-darkened face that made her foolish heart tumble. "You're one stubborn woman, Doc. Okay, let's go."

This time he used the bikes and quads for balance, moving forward like a drunken sailor, but still moving. And then, just like that, their avenue of escape was cut off. A bright flare of orange flame twirled with a plume of black smoke in a ghastly dance, filling the doorway.

Sam crumbled, defeated. The beast had won after all.

———

MAC STARED at the wall of flames, his jaw clenched in fury. It was one thing for the bastards to come after him, but Sam didn't deserve this. He gingerly touched the back of his head and cursed his stupidity. The goose egg was a timely reminder; these people meant business. He blinked the cobwebs away and searched hopelessly for an escape route. Damn it, other than a narrow window—he'd never fit—high up on the wall over the tool bench, they were well and truly trapped. At least he could save Sam, that was something.

He sat on the skidoo seat to give his knee a break and gather strength for what was to come, and that's when he noticed it—keys. He reached over and, holding his breath, fired the snow machine up. It coughed a couple of times before catching, the engine giving a satisfying rev when he hit the gas.

He gazed triumphantly at Sam. "Your chariot awaits, miss."

She looked at him like he'd lost his common sense. "Are you nuts?" She waved a hand around the smoking room. "There's no way out of here. We're going to die."

Tears stood out in her blue eyes and sent a knife to

his heart. She'd been so courageous, braving the fire to save his worthless ass. If it was the last thing he did, he'd get her out of here safely.

And then he was going to make his enemies pay.

"Do you trust me?" he asked, uncomfortably aware how important her response was. When she slowly nodded, his chest swelled. "Okay. I need you to wrap that tarp there over your head and then climb on behind me and hang on. Can you do that?"

Damn, he wished he'd kept his truck keys in his pocket instead of on the hall table under his wife's picture. There was nothing for it, he had to work with the tools he'd been given. Eyes and throat burning, head throbbing, and knee aching, he still found room to smile at the little red riding hood using his shoulder for balance as she snuggled in behind him—and damn, didn't that feel good. She wrapped her arms around his waist, and he closed his eyes for a moment to take in the exquisite sensation, before covering her hands with one of his. "No matter what, don't let go. Ready?"

He felt her nod against his back.

Okay, this is it. Focus, Wanowski. Straight to the offensive zone.

He heard his wife's words in his head and warmth suffused his body. His growing feelings for the woman behind him had left a guilty pit in his gut, but Jess's guiding spirit reassured him. Maybe the past and the present *could* meld together—if they survived.

One last squeeze of Sam's fingers, damn, they were cold, and he snapped the machine into gear and twisted the handle full-throttle.

Sam's scream reverberated in his eardrums along with the screech of steel tracks grabbing for traction on the cement floor. Between one heartbeat and the next, the skidoo torpedoed straight for the burning garage doors. Flames had weakened the wood, but he'd still be lucky if it gave under the snow mobile's skis. At the very last second, Mac ducked his head and threw an arm behind himself to grasp Sam's back, gluing her body to his. The skidoo hit the wall with the force of an explosion, wood, smoke and flames shooting everywhere.

And then they were free, bursting into the sparkling, cold night air and sailing down the road with the wind in their hair and Mac's lips turned up in a grin of sheer triumph.

They'd done it.

11

THE SATELLITE PHONE RANG. Hewett looked at his partner and shrugged. "Better answer it, man. The boss don't like to be kept waiting."

Roberts snorted, but reached for the handset anyway. "Yeah."

"Report." The voice on the other end demanded respect.

Roberts rolled down the driver's side window and spit into the wind and snow before rolling it up to answer. "We took care of him. He won't be bothering you no more."

"You better be right. If not..."

Roberts scowled and flipped the wipers to high. "I said it's done."

"Watch your mouth, *boy*. Where do you think

you're going now? I never said you could leave the area."

Christ. Roberts took the handset away from his ear and stared at it. The asshole was tracking them.

"What's going on?" Hewett asked, his bald head gleaming in the lights of the dashboard.

"Nothing." Roberts lifted the phone to his ear again. "There's a freaking blizzard and you expect us to stay on this mountain?"

"I *expect* you to do what I paid you to do," the boss growled. "I can't afford mistakes, and neither can you. Ride out the storm and then go back and make sure you did your job. Understand?"

Roberts smacked the steering wheel, then had to work fast to correct the tires as they skidded on the icy roads. This was nothing but bullshit. When he got back to town… Yeah, okay. Nothing would happen. He liked his skin right where it was, but shit.

"Storm's supposed to last a couple of days. I'll get back to you after."

"You'd better. You really don't want to piss me off." The boss ended the call and Roberts tossed the phone onto the seat amid the pile of fast food wrappers they'd been subsisting on. Just fun-fucking-tastic.

REALITY QUICKLY SET IN. Now the adrenaline had worn off, Mac's headache returned with a vengeance. Neither of them had left the house with coats, instead focused on stopping the fire before any real damage was done.

He slowed the snowmobile and turned back toward the cabin. The storm was picking up intensity, the blizzard hurling snow at the burning garage like nature's fire brigade. It was too late to save the building, but at least the forest stood a chance.

He killed the engine and glanced over his shoulder. "Cold?" Sam was practically vibrating, eyes glassy from shock.

"Frozen," she confirmed, her gaze on the dancing flames. "Is the house far enough away?"

He sincerely hoped so. "We need shelter, and since this is our only form of transportation now, warmer clothing."

She nodded and then her eyes went wide as she took in his words. "Wait. What do you mean, this is our only transportation? We can call Uncle Thomas, he'll come for us." Even as she spoke, her shoulders slumped. "The storm. There's no phone service. Can't we just wait it out? The fire is slowing down, we should be safe." She released her stranglehold on his waist and hugged herself, shivering.

The goose egg on his noggin said otherwise. The

forest was deceptively calm now. The snow layered everything in a carpet of peace, seeming to snuff out the evil that lurked on its borders. But he knew better.

Sam rose and left a chill in her wake. Mac bemoaned the loss of her thighs wrapped around his, it made him wish for a warm bed and a willing woman. This woman.

There were no tracks leading up to the door this time, but he still held her back, entering first with his fists at the ready.

Sam noticed his tense posture and frowned. "You don't think that fire was an accident, do you?"

Wordless, he turned and gingerly moved the hair on his scalp, showing her the injured area.

She gasped. Her cold fingers brushed his aside for a better look. "What happened?" she asked, her breath sending prickles down his back.

He shrugged and moved away, irritated with his body's instant reaction to her touch. "Someone got the drop on me in the garage. Cracked me over the head and then started that fire to shut me up for good, I guess." He hesitated, then decided she had the right to know. "The phone line was deliberately cut as well. That's why we can't call out."

Fear darkened her eyes, even as she stiffened her spine. "We aren't stranded, we have the skidoo."

Mac wanted to enfold her in his arms. She was

strong, his therapist. "That's right, we do. And the storm is on our side. No one's going to be getting around in this sh... stuff. By the time they come back— if that's their intention—we'll be long gone."

Her brows drew together. "Who are they, Mac? Do you have any idea?" Now that they were in the relative warmth of the house, goose bumps had erupted all over her arms and did interesting things to the front of her shirt. Catching his gaze, she covered her breasts with folded arms. "Let's go sit by the fire to talk. I'm frozen."

He was a dog—thinking about sex when they were in dire straits. She was just so... perfect. It was impossible to ignore the chemistry between them—at least for him it was. She didn't seem to be afflicted by the same attraction.

Disgruntled, he followed her down the hall to the toasty den. The fire had all but burned itself out, but the coals still smoldered in the grate. He added another log, aware that Sam had curled onto a corner of the couch. When he turned, it was to see her staring out the window. "Don't worry, the snow will put out the flames."

Her decidedly lopsided smile drew him to the sofa. She tipped her head, and her damp blond hair fell over her shoulder and curled under her breast. "We're in big trouble, aren't we? Don't lie, I can handle it, really I can." Tears overflowed and the next thing he knew she'd thrown herself into his arms. "I'm so... sorry, it's just that we didn't get along, and then someone shot at us, and then we were getting along, and then the garage started on fire and someone tried to kill you, and... I'm so confused," she wailed.

Mac smiled against her forehead and breathed in the mix of smoke and fresh air that clung to her skin. The thought of what could have happened straightened his lips into more of a grimace. What if she'd walked into the garage while those goons were still there? It didn't bear thinking about. "Shh, it's going to be all right, I promise. Tomorrow, we'll head down the mountain and get you back home where you'll be safe. Then, I'll go to the police with our complaints and let them find those creeps." He planted a gentle kiss on her cheekbone, just under her eye and tasted the salt of her tears. Tenderness was replaced with hunger. He tipped her head for better access and groaned aloud at the moist lushness of her mouth.

"Sam, open your eyes, honey. I want... no, I need to kiss you now. Please tell me that's okay." His heart stuttered at the beautiful woman in his arms. Her wet lashes were thick and dark and highlighted the Caribbean blue intensity of her gaze. Her skin, porcelain smooth and perfect, right down to the little mole near the corner of her mouth, invited him to touch. Caress. Her body, melded to his chest, curved into his like it belonged—two sides of a whole. At the first taste, his pulse leaped. He tightened his hold and breathed her name, gratified when she melted into his arms. His lips moved over hers, feeding on the sweet taste unique to Sam. He cupped a smooth cheek, her damp hair cool against the back of his hand, her mouth hot and honeyed. The cream-colored blouse clung to her supple body, nipples hard, demanding his touch. Her fingers drifted over his lower torso and his hips surged, helpless against her allure. Mac groaned, frustrated with the clothes and the distance between them.

He leaned back and closed his eyes, chest heaving.

"That was...," she murmured.

He turned his head to look at her and damn near pulled her onto his lap. Her mussed hair, swollen lips, and transparent shirt undid him. "Not a mistake, if that's what you're thinking."

"I was going to say a surprise," she answered, sitting up and straightening her clothes. "And it can't happen again." He stiffened and her gaze flitted to his lips and away again. "We're working together, Mac. It's too..."

"Complicated?" he supplied sarcastically. As though everything that had happened between them wasn't problematic. If they were equally invested, they could figure it out, but he wasn't going to beg. Obviously, the job meant more to her than he did.

She lowered her hands to her lap and twisted her fingers together. "There's something I need to..."

He rose, refusing to hear her end their relationship before she gave him a chance. "I'm tired," he said abruptly. "Get some sleep. We leave at dawn." Knee aching almost as much as his heart, he turned and strode upstairs.

12

SAM TOSSED and turned the night away and woke up sore and out of sorts. She sat up and dangled her feet over the edge of the oversized bed. She wished she could speak with her uncle. She wanted—needed—to tell Mac the truth, even though she'd been warned to keep quiet. He had a right to know. If only it wasn't a condition of her pending contract with the team. This position could cement her future, did she really want to chance giving that up for a guy who acted like he couldn't wait to get rid of her half of the time? But then there were those other moments—like last night.

Just thinking about his lips on hers made the reflection staring back at her from the mirror above the black lacquer dresser turn soft and dewy eyed. Not good. Not good at all. After her relationship with Jeff last year, she'd promised herself she was going to focus on her career. Her mom worried. She wanted her daughter to have security, and since Sam disagreed that safety meant a husband and two-point-five children, she was determined to make her business a success.

Cleo nudged the unlatched door open and glided across the room to hop gracefully onto the bed and rub her silky head under Sam's arm.

"Hello, sweetheart. Where's your daddy, huh? I hope you have a cat carrier because we have to make a trip today and I'm not leaving you behind."

"I'm *not* her father, and there's no room for a carrier on the skidoo. You do remember that's our mode of transportation, don't you?" Mac leaned against the doorjamb in a worn pair of jeans—torn at the knee—and nothing else.

Sam's mouth dried. Did he have to look that good first thing in the morning? She cleared her throat and went on the defensive. "It's courteous to knock before entering a lady's bedroom. What if I slept in the nude?" *Oops, too much information.*

Mac's gaze turned distinctly predatory. He slowly straightened and stalked across the room, every bit as sleek and pantherish as his cat. His legs bumped hers as he leaned into her space, the rough material of his jeans sending a shiver of longing up her spine. "If you were naked, we wouldn't be having this discussion right now," he murmured, then proceeded to box her in with his hands bracketing her hips to make his point.

Cleo meowed her displeasure, twitched her tail, and hopped off the mattress, landing on the hardwood floor with barely a sound.

Sam wished she could do the same. Instead, this... buffoon with his six pack abs and mesmerizing eyes— gray-blue with a dark ring around the iris—had decided to make her his morning distraction. She shoved his chest, briefly closing her fingers over the smooth musculature of his skin. "Get off me, Wanowski. If you're feeling so much better this morning, I'm going to assume you've already turned on the coffee machine because I don't do *anything* without coffee."

The bugger had the temerity to grin at her. "Who would have figured such a prissy female could have claws?" he mused.

Prissy? Organized, yes. Maybe even goal-orientated, but no one had ever accused her of being straitlaced before. Sam pushed past the annoying jerk, her cheeks hot. "If you're finished making fun of me, please leave my room. I want to get dressed." She stood by the door, the knob digging into her back, aware of Mac with every fiber of her being.

He raised his hands, palms up. "Whoa, take it easy, Doc. No need to get your panties in a twist." His gaze sobered. "Look, yesterday was rough. I'm sorry you had to go through that." He brushed a lock of messy hair behind her ear and smiled. "Did you know your eyes flash when you're upset?"

She frowned, skin tingling where he'd touched her. "I'm not upset. I *am* uncomfortable with having a strange man in my bedroom. So, if you don't mind—" She cringed on the inside. She sounded just like the prudish woman he accused her of being.

He straightened and took a step back. "I don't know what you've heard, but most hockey players are good guys. They have wives, kids, some even do charity work. I'm not about to force myself on you, if that's what you're thinking."

Now she felt foolish. Of course he wouldn't try anything with her. He could have any beautiful ice bunny he wanted, while she was just... normal. Oh, her parts were all in the right place, and she'd been told she had nice eyes, but it wasn't enough to hold the attention of someone like Wanowski. He was out of her league. Literally, if she couldn't nail down this contract. Which meant keeping her reasons for being there quiet for just a little while longer.

"Maybe we should stay here. Wait out the storm and then get help. It seems foolhardy to go racing down a mountain on a motorized sled in the middle of a blizzard." She folded her arms and tried not to think about her bare legs under the thigh-length nightie she'd worn to bed.

Mac shook his head and flicked a finger under her chin. "We're leaving in an hour. The snow has let up and I want to get a head start before the next cell moves in. Whoever dinged me last night and started the shed on fire is dangerous. I'm not willing to risk you getting hurt—end of story." He limped a few feet down the hall before glancing over his shoulder. "Wear something warmer than what you have on. It's winter, princess."

Before she could think up a suitable retort, he was gone. Ooh, that man. She stomped her foot, then gave the door a satisfying slam. Too bad the darn thing closed with a soft whoomph. He was *the* most aggravating, irritating, exasperating person she'd ever had the misfortune to meet. Her shoulders slumped. She had no choice, he was determined to leave. They were going to ride that deathtrap he called a skidoo, unless...

The thought of pretending an illness she didn't have in front of Mac's all-seeing eyes, made her tummy flip. Maybe she wouldn't be faking after all.

By THE TIME Sam wound up her courage enough to dress *appropriately,* as she'd been ordered, and made her way downstairs, Mac had already packed a couple of army green canvas duffle bags and stacked them by the door.

She followed the scent of fresh-brewed coffee to the kitchen where he stood gazing out the window over the sink at the frozen vista beyond. She took a moment to admire the perfect symmetry of the broad back tapering to a lean waist and long, powerful legs before he turned and caught her stare. *God, you're a beautiful man.* The ambient light filtering through the glass turned his hair into a warm gold halo surrounding a face Michelangelo would have loved to capture. Her fingers itched to trace the sharp planes of his cheek bones, the jut of his jaw, the shape of his brow. The feel of his lips. She'd never been so instantly attracted to a man. He wasn't even her type. She leaned more toward scholarly types—men who used their brains instead of brawn. Not that she had any doubt Mac was smart. It was just that he was so much more. The whole package.

"Coffee?"

"Huh?" she asked, dazed. "Ah, sure. I mean, yes. Please." Could she be any more obvious?

He gave her a quizzical look, then poured a mug from the carafe beside the sink. "Enjoy. It'll be the last one we get for a while." He passed it over and she accepted, careful their fingers didn't touch.

"I still think this is a bad idea," Sam muttered into her cup. "And, besides… I'm not feeling so great. I think my friend is coming to visit, if you know what I mean."

"Your friend?" Mac questioned.

She rubbed at her fluttering tummy and tried to quell the blush suffusing her cheeks. It was almost comical when he finally caught on. His eyes grew wide and he backed himself into the counter as though her supposed affliction was contagious, or something. She would have laughed if it wasn't so embarrassing—and a lie, which made it even worse.

"Well, um, if we head out soon, before the next storm hits, we should be off the mountain before… you know." He waved toward her midsection, his gaze bouncing from her face to the door as though he couldn't wait to escape.

Well, join the party. Desperate times called for desperate measures. She squared her shoulders and lifted her chin. "It's too late. I can't leave."

He stared at her, his gaze incredulous. "Are you telling me just because you have your period—yes, I know what that is, even if you can't say the damn word —you're going to force us to stay in this cabin? You do realize that fire is just the beginning, right? Whatever those goons want, they aren't going to stop until they get it." He brushed a frustrated hand through wavy hair and cursed. "Christ, Sam, you drive me crazy." He stomped out of the room, his bad leg dragging only a little behind his temper.

She sagged onto the nearest chair. Well, she'd won this round, but when he found out the truth he was going to feel so betrayed. Good thing she wasn't invested in their relationship, he didn't strike her as an understanding type of guy.

Sighing, she rose to place her cup in the sink and caught a glimpse of the charred remains of the garage through the trees. She shivered from a chill that had nothing to do with the weather.

13

Mac attacked the pile of wood outside, turning thick chunks of hemlock and cedar into little more than kindling. That woman couldn't see common sense if it was written on her forehead. Surely, she had to understand it was a mistake to remain here. They were defenseless. He was The Hammer—his inability to protect Sam grated like hell.

Growling under his breath, he buried the axe into the chopping block and bent to collect an armful of the aromatic sticks. The snow started to fall again, swiftly coating his hair and creeping down the back of his neck. The temperature had dropped as well, and his breath made a foggy cloud in front of his face. The snow crunched under his work boots, the sound an eerie accompaniment to the wind whistling in the woods.

This is ridiculous. Why was he letting a city slicker therapist decide their fate? What happened to the hard-nosed hockey player that never allowed anyone to walk over him? His teammates would laugh their asses off if they could see him now.

Or envy him.

It had taken everything he had to remain at the kitchen window this morning instead of finishing what he'd started upstairs. She'd made him burn from the inside out with little more than a kiss. When he thought of what they could have got up to on that neat and tidy bed of hers... he had to rearrange his junk.

She was stubborn, he'd give her that, but she'd never make a poker player. There was no hiding her embarrassment over her womanly functions, but she'd brazened it out, determined to keep them there, at the cabin.

The question was why.

He'd find it funny if it wasn't so serious. The gunshots, the lump on his head and the burned out remains of his truck were all the proof he needed. The danger was real.

Another why.

He added the wood to the stack by the back door and heaved out a disgruntled breath. He didn't want to connect Sam to whatever was going on in his life, but the evidence was lining up and he wasn't an idiot. He watched the snow swirl for a few minutes. At least they wouldn't end up possibly lost on the mountain if they stayed. Silver linings. He'd acted as though he could get them down with no problem, but truthfully, without the road or GPS as guidance, he wasn't so sure. And then there was his knee. He flexed the joint, relieved when there was barely more than a spasm. Still, a two or three hour skidoo ride over bumpy terrain wouldn't do it any favors. He glanced over to where he'd hidden the machine under a tarp found in the duffle bags he'd unearthed from Samson's closet. The snow was helping his cause, the whole thing little more than a dark lump now. Sam could have her two days while the storm raged and then they were leaving, one way or the other.

He opened the door and entered the back porch off the kitchen. In the summer, he could envision the small chamber as a breakfast nook overlooking the lake below. He envied his buddy this sanctuary. A place to leave the chaos of their sport behind—to regroup. Mac had been running in overdrive since Jess's death; at first to outrun the pain, and then later, the memories. The tranquil atmosphere of the mountains seeped into his bones, giving him the first taste of peace he'd enjoyed in a long time.

A soft murmur turned his gaze from the outdoors to the interior. At first, he thought Sam was chatting to the cat, but Cleo chose that moment to make an appearance in the doorway, head tipped curiously.

"Has she taken up talking to herself now?" he asked the cat. Cleo meowed and led the way through the kitchen, tail pointing at the second floor. Mac kicked off his snow-covered boots and followed on stocking feet, surprised to find Sam on her cell phone in the den. She sat on the window seat, a book in hand and blond hair creating a curtain over her face. He opened his mouth to ask about the cell service but hesitated at the mention of his name.

"Mac deserves to know, Uncle. Please, I can't do this for much longer." She threw the book onto the cushions and stood, her gaze widening on Mac. "Umm, I have to go. Think about what I said, okay? See you soon." Her smile looked forced as she lifted her phone in the air. "I decided to give it another try, and voilà —service."

Mac's bullshit meter crossed the red line. What the hell was going on? Did she have coverage the whole time? He hadn't considered it after his own cell failed. Surely, she would have said something after the fire. None of this made sense.

He helped himself to a two-finger serving of Donaldson's whiskey, the hard liquor searing his throat. She touched his shoulder and he recoiled, slamming the glass onto the bar. "Don't. You've been playing me, Doc, and I don't like it. I don't like it at all."

Sam frowned, hurt and something less defined flitting across her expression. "I thought you'd be happy. We can get out of here now. Uncle Thomas is sending a car tomorrow, as soon as the next storm front passes through. That's good news, isn't it?"

Sure. If she was telling the truth.

"What did you want to tell me?" he asked abruptly, swinging around to rest an elbow on the bar.

She stared at him, her gaze puzzled. "I'm not sure I know what you mean."

The phone rested on the counter between them—a ticking time bomb. "I heard you, Samantha." She winced at the use of her full name. "You told your uncle I deserved to know what's going on. I couldn't agree more, so talk."

She lowered her eyes, hiding from him. "It's... nothing. I just wanted to let you know how well your treatment is coming, and Uncle Thomas wanted me to wait until he can explain it as your doctor." She grasped his arm and looked at him with deceiving blue eyes. "You should be happy, Mac. You won't need an operation. You'll be able to return to the game by next season, for sure."

Next season.

He jerked away from her touch, anger carrying him

across the room. "What about *this* season, Doc? I've worked my ass off to get where I am, and you're telling me my chances for the cup have gone down the drain?" He swore and punched the mantle over the fireplace, barely aware of the skin breaking on his knuckles. "What the hell did I hire you for? You've been nothing but trouble since you arrived. I'll be *happy*, as you so eloquently put it, to get off this mountain and never see you again. That's the *only* thing I'm looking forward to right now."

He turned to glare in her direction. She wavered like a sapling in a wind storm, her eyes jewel-bright against the pallor of her face. Guilt broadsided him. Damn his hotheaded temper. What if he'd been wrong?

"Sam," he said, and took an awkward step forward.

"No." She lifted a trembling hand and backed away. "I think you've said enough, thank you. I... I'll be in my room—packing. Let me know when the car arrives." She turned and walked away, her back ramrod straight. He'd hurt her. And the damnable part of it was, he was the one left aching.

14

Sam threw the last of her clothes into the over-flowing suitcase laying open on the bed, then attempted to close the lid, but no amount of pushing and shoving would get the darn zipper to move. Frustrated, and near tears, she rolled off the bulging bag and stared at the ceiling. She wasn't used to people yelling at her the way *he* had. Her family treated her like a princess—more so after her father died—which fueled her hunger to be independent and succeed in her chosen field. And, as to the men in her life, up to now, she'd been the aggressor. The one to break things off before they became serious. She had a plan; career first, family later—much later.

She pulled a downy pillow close and hugged it to her chest. Why did it matter if Mac hated her? Because, she'd failed. That's all this was. His therapy and the request from the coach was her chance to fast-track her business into a secure position and she'd ruined it. It had nothing to do with whether she liked the man or not—at this moment, most definitely *not*—it was business.

And she was the Princess of Monaco, too.

They had a connection. The air practically vibrated with electricity every time they were in a room together. If he wanted to deny their attraction and pretend nothing had happened, so be it. She could accept that, it was probably for the best.

If only it didn't hurt so much.

Her heart jumped at a knock on the door.

"Sam, can I come in for a minute? We should talk."

She turned her head and stared at the door. "I think we've said it all, Wanowski. Go away."

The knob rattled. "Come on, Doc. You owe me."

She entertained the thought of ignoring him until he gave up, but he was right—damn him. She cast the pillow aside and stood, brushing the moisture from beneath her eyes as she strode to the door. A long inhale and slow exhale later, she unlocked and opened the door. Mac stood there with hunched shoulders and hands in the pockets of worn jeans. Her pulse skipped a beat.

"This isn't a good time." She glanced at the mess on her bed. "I'm busy."

He put a palm on the door she'd started to close. "Let me in, Sam. Please."

Sure she was making a mistake, but helpless to turn him away, Sam stepped into the room and nervously began to fold the clothes in her suitcase. "What do you want, Mac, an apology in blood? I already explained…"

He took the satiny underwear out of her hand and tossed it aside, before turning her to face him. "As you may have noticed, I have a tendency to talk before I think. It gets me in all kinds of shit, believe me." He smiled, but it faded when she didn't respond. He tipped her chin up and frowned at the obvious signs of her distress. "Is that because of me?"

She snorted and jerked free. "Don't flatter yourself. I'm catching a cold, it makes my eyes water." No way was she going to admit he'd hurt her feelings. Tired of keeping the truth from him, Sam perched on the edge of the mattress and fidgeted with the zipper on her suitcase. "There's something you should probably know—" she peeped at him through her lashes, caught his sudden stillness, and looked away, "—when your coach hired me to come out here and care for you, it was with the stipulation that I slow down your therapy."

"Have you no conscience?" He grasped her wrists and gave them a shake. "That's my livelihood and you're treating it as though it's a game to you."

She tensed at his growing anger and hurried to

correct his misconceptions. "To keep you from rein-juring your knee. That's all, I swear." His fingers cut into her wrists like a set of manacles. He was scaring her. "Let go, Mac, you're hurting me."

He immediately loosened his grip, his eyes contrite when he noticed the reddened skin. "God, Sam, I'm sorry. I would never intentionally..."

She cupped his jaw, the golden-brown stubble tick-ling her fingertips. "Shh, you don't have to apologize. I should have explained it better. I have the upmost respect for what you do out on that ice and if you ever saw me on skates, you'd know why." She smiled, then realized how close they were and dropped her hand. "Physiotherapy is a two-way street, Mac. It can only work if the patient is onboard with the treatment."

He couldn't seem to look away from his finger-prints on her arms. He took her hand in his and lifted it to his mouth. She gasped as his lips feathered over the hollow of her wrist, the touch soothing and erotic at the same time.

"So soft," he whispered, his breath raising goose bumps along her spine. "Why is it I can't keep my hands off of you?" he mused. "You exasperate me almost as much as you turn me on."

Sam barely heard him, her attention entirely focused on those lips and what they were doing to her pulse. She whimpered and he smiled against her skin.

Cheeks fiery, she tried to yank her arm free, but he was having none of it. Instead, he wrapped her hands behind his neck and traced a line of kisses along her arm, leaving a trail of fire in his wake.

"I think I'm going to have to kiss you," he murmured, his gaze on her tingling lips.

She let out a shaky breath. "I don't think that's a good—" He dipped his head and their mouths met. She was pretty sure there were sparks involved. A deep, almost involuntary groan seemed to rise from his chest and now she was the one smiling against his lips.

He tipped his head back far enough to meet her gaze, his own eyes hooded. Hot. "What's so funny?"

She shrugged, warm under the heat of his regard. "When I get nervous, I laugh. It's an involuntary reaction to overloaded stimuli..." The words petered out at his bemused expression.

"Are you saying I make you uneasy, Doc?" he grinned. His big hands slid down her arms and rested on the bed, forcing her to lie down or bump faces. Mac's smile grew in triumph. "You were saying?"

Holy Batman. Talk about sensory overloads. The scent of cedar clung to his clothes, a perfect accent to his overwhelming masculinity. The forearms bracketing her shoulders—bared by rolled up sleeves—bulged with a latent strength that made her girly parts quiver. She bit her lip and tried not to squirm, but he picked up on her tell, his gaze narrowing on her mouth.

"You tempt me, woman. You're dangerous," he muttered, just before seeking her lips again. He licked the spot she'd worried with her teeth, the sensation causing her heart to stutter. "Open for me, Sam," he whispered.

And she did.

MAC WOKE to a dark room and a sleeping blond blanket. Sam had draped herself over his chest, her cheek resting against his heart and their legs entwined. He lay there for a moment breathing in the scent of their passion. A sense of rightness filled his chest. She was perfect. Never before had he laughed during sex, but Sam's quirky humor had turned the intimacy into something more than affection. Tenderness for the woman in his arms tightened his throat. He was falling for Samantha Walters.

He brushed the messy hair away and pressed a kiss to her forehead, smiling when she murmured a protest and cuddled closer. Her full breasts nestled his ribs, triggering a response he wouldn't have thought possible after the night they had just shared. She was incredibly responsive, keen, receptive. They were good together.

He wanted to see her after this was over. He hadn't even asked about her job or where she lived—whether there was another man in her life. The last thought soured his stomach and he cast it aside. Besides, it wasn't like they'd promised undying love before hooking up. Free agents and all that. Like his career at the end of this season. He was looking at an empty future without the playoffs. Shit, he was older than half the guys on the team and had the battle scars to prove it. The scouts were always on the search for the next big thing—his days were numbered, and he would have been fine with that if he could have ended in a blaze of glory. Instead of the dream of having his number retired, he was going to end up a has-been player looking for coaching jobs, or God help him, a sports caster.

What would Sam think of him then?

He ran his hand down the length of her hip, the bare skin soft and supple with an underlying thread of steel that reminded him of her personality. She flexed and stretched, welcoming his touch even as she moaned at getting drawn from her rest.

"Hey, Sleeping Beauty. Time to wake up, you've put my arm to sleep," he teased. He gave her backside a light slap and she squealed, sitting up in a rush, boobs bouncing and hair flying every which way. Mac grinned, enjoying the view.

She stared down at him indignantly. "That was rude, mister. If that's how you treat all your lady friends—" Her nose scrunched up adorably. "—it's no wonder you're single." Her eyes widened. "You *are* single, aren't you?"

He tucked his arms behind his head, the better to take in the fire he'd stirred. "A little late to ask me that now, isn't it? I could ask you the same." He waited for her to reassure him,

And waited.

Instead, she rolled out of bed and eyed their love nest as though it contained a nest of scorpions. She waved a hand up and down the length of his rather impressive body, if he did say so himself, but kept her gaze on his face. "You... I... this was a mistake." She looked so distressed he was tempted to take her in his arms, but damn, he didn't much like where she was headed with this.

"What do you mean, a mistake?" he said, sitting up and casually bending his good leg so his foot could rest on the inner thigh of the other leg. Her gaze landed on his growing erection and she glared like it was all his fault—hey, he was a guy, sue him.

"You know darn well why," she snapped. "I'm employed by your boss. It's... unethical."

He snorted. "Babe, if you think this is wrong, you should see what happens on a road trip." He sighed, aware he was burying himself deeper. "Look, as long as *I'm* not your boss, it's a non-issue. You're making too big a deal out of this."

She frowned and crossed her arms under her *bare* breasts. He almost went cross-eyed and lost his train of thought. "Easy for you to say, it's not your job on the line. You have it made with your multi-million-dollar career goofing off chasing a puck on the ice. Some of us have real responsibilities." She covered her mouth, as though realizing what she'd said. "Mac, that's not what..."

Now it was his turn to get upset. What gave her the right to judge him? He'd worked every bit as hard as she had for his dream. He should have known she wouldn't understand—she wasn't his type. "Come back to bed, honeybun. We get along better when we're doing dirt, than when we talk. Let's skip right to the good stuff." He lay back and rolled his hips, trying to be as obnoxious as she seemed to think athletes were— which begged the question, why was she even helping him?

She stared at him with a mix of hurt and disgust, then turned without another word, and walked into the bathroom, closing the door with a too-quiet click.

Guess the honeymoon was over.

15

COACH GLARED at the idiot powering his way down the ice as though the rest of his team weren't waiting in the wings for the pass he was *supposed* to make. How many times did he have to go over this shit before they listened?

"Pass the puck," he yelled, along with the players warming the bench in front of him. "Idiot," he growled as the forward from the opposing team scooped it and raced the other way—*passing the puck*. And since all the WarHawks were on the other end, which left their goalie guarding the net on his own, it only took a couple of fast maneuvers and they scored.

Game over.

Aware the cameras were focused on him, Dan kept a stoic expression while inside his guts burned. If they kept this up, the team wouldn't make the playoffs and if they didn't make the playoffs he was screwed. *How had he let himself get into this mess?*

The teams met at center ice. The WarHawks yanked a glove off and shook hands with the winners, one by one. His guys were tired, frustrated, and quickly losing hope. Maybe he shouldn't have gotten rid of Wanowski so soon. Too late—what was done, was done. All he could do now was damage control.

He carefully straightened his crumpled tie and headed down the narrow hallway leading to the dressing rooms, dragging his heels on the rubber flooring. Normally, the musty, sweaty, icy perfume created by the Zamboni soothed the tension that followed him like a shadow, but today it did nothing to dispel his fears. One more game. After that they were out of the standings and their shot at the cup was over. Not that they could be allowed to win anyway, but he had to make it look good for the big money to drop. His life depended on it.

"Good game."

Dan turned and waited for Doc to catch up. His friend sported a few more gray hairs every time he saw him—hell, so did he. They were two dinosaurs in a sea of faces that seemed to get younger with every season. Well, after this year he could retire in style. He just had to get through the next couple of months.

"What was so great about it? We lost." He folded his arms over a barrel chest. His kid ragged on him to exercise more, try the Keto diet that was all the rage—until the next big fad came along—but he wasn't having it. He liked a cold beer and a big steak, and he didn't see himself giving it up for that salad crap.

Doc rubbed a grizzled jaw. "Well, that's true enough, but our boys made them work for it. Did you see that move by Lazlo? He blocked three guys until Donaldson could get by and score. No one gets past that Croatian." He chuckled.

It was true. The WarHawks were a formidable team. The key players, including Wanowski, had played together for a long time—they operated like a well-oiled machine. He had a feeling that was part of the problem tonight, they missed their captain. They better get over it; they were up against the best in the league next week.

The locker room was subdued—a stark contrast to victory celebrations. Towels littered the floor, B.O. blended with the fresh scent of soap from the showers, and men chatted half-heartedly while changing into street clothes.

Guilt made Dan's voice harsh. "What the hell was going on out there? You pansy-asses know what side of the ice you're supposed to be protecting? 'Cause I wasn't seeing it." He slammed a locker door shut and the room went silent. "You screwed up tonight." He stared each man down, daring them to argue. When they remained silent, morose, he sighed and did his job. "That's okay, everyone has an off-night, but we can't have a repeat next week or we're done. You got that?"

"Ya, Coach. We try harder next time," Lazlo assured him. "Will Wanowski be back before the playoffs?"

Dan cursed under his breath and ignored the questioning glance from Doc. "Just worry about your game. I'll handle Wanowski." *Literally.* The guy was a thorn in his side.

Doc clapped the Slavic's back. "My niece is his therapist, Hans. She assured me just yesterday that he's almost fully recovered and will be back in plenty of time for the next game."

Dan frowned. Why hadn't he heard anything about this? What the hell was he paying those two idiots for if they couldn't even take care of one beat-up, has-been hockey player? "I thought the storms were too bad to go up the mountain?" he asked. Hewett had assured him no one was moving in the blizzard conditions. And besides, Wanowski's truck was little more than scrap metal after the fire.

"You need to get out of the playbooks and watch the news, Coach." Donaldson's smile was grim as though he knew something, but no, that wasn't possible. Was it?

"There's a two day break in the storm front, so I'm going up tomorrow to bring Sam home," Doc said, and shot a reprimanding glance to the defenseman who shrugged and turned away to rummage in his locker for a shirt.

A growl crawled its way up Dan's throat and threatened to erupt into a full-blown snarl. Did he have to handle everything himself? *This is the last time.* He didn't care if the mob took out his other knee, he wasn't doing this shit again.

He forced a hey-good-buddy grin and threw an arm over Doc's shoulders. "We don't need to fly out until Friday, I'll come with you, check out this mansion in the hills Samson keeps bragging about." He shot a shark's smile at Donaldson. "You boys can spend the time practicing—you need it."

Thomas nodded, his expression uncertain. "Sure, if you can spare the time. It's a fair drive from here, you sure you can handle it?" He glanced meaningfully at Coach's knee.

Dan dropped his arm from his friend's shoulder and bit back the retort on his lips. "I want to get a look at Wanowski myself, make sure he's ready to play. I can't afford to have an injured man on the ice, and I don't put it past The Hammer to trick his way into a game. The guy has no boundaries."

"That's because he's a team player," Donaldson retorted. "He knows how important this is—to *all* of us."

Coach snorted and then bore the wrath of their glares. They had no idea.

16

By the time Sam showered, blow-dried her hair, dressed in blue jeans and a cream turtleneck sweater, and added make-up to cover blotchy skin, she figured the bozo she'd just made love with would have had the sense to leave her room.

And she was right.

Instead of the relief she should feel, all she noticed was the void he left. Mac had filled every nook and cranny with his forceful personality; he was a hard man to ignore.

Drawn to the bed where they'd lain together, she cuddled the downy pillow to her chest and buried her nose in the indent created by his head. It brought back every heated moment. His husky voice, her fingers combing through thick brown hair, the feel of his lips on her breast. Impossible to deny the lust he'd drawn from her without effort. And if he walked through that door right now, she'd do it all again, too. He was her kryptonite, but they lived in different worlds.

It could never work.

She reluctantly replaced the pillow on the bed and straightened the covers over rumpled sheets. Her career, home and family meant everything, while Mac traveled extensively and barely mentioned anything personal. Then again, if she managed to somehow land the hockey therapist contract, she'd have to follow the team from game to game as well. It was something to consider before accepting the position. After her dad's sudden death, Mom had floundered for a long time, then turned overprotective. Sam winced. She should have called while she had reception. Hopefully, Uncle Thomas had thought to reassure her mother. He'd been a godsend these past few months since the accident. She couldn't have managed without him. None of them could have. Her father had been a hard worker, but, like too many, hadn't planned for his death and left his family in financial ruin. If not for Uncle Thomas, Mom would have had to sell her home, Kevin couldn't have continued in college and she would have given up her degree. They owed everything to Mom's brother.

She lifted the overturned suitcase that had fallen off the end of the bed earlier when she and Mac... Just thinking about the things she'd done with the hockey player warmed Sam's cheeks and made her heart skip. She'd had boyfriends before, but none so flagrantly... male. He reminded her of a lion; proud, strong, arrogant—sensual. No wonder they called him *The Hammer,* he'd certainly pounded her sensible nature into the bed sheets. She grinned foolishly.

A crash, followed by some creative swearing sent her sprinting for the door, pulse thundering in her chest. She took the stairs too fast and tripped, but caught the banister in time to save her fall. Slowing long enough to catch her breath, Sam hurried down the dark hall to the only room with a light—the kitchen.

Mac stood shirtless, in a pair of jeans, near the center island, his gaze on the shattered picture frame lying dangerously close to bare feet. His lips twisted in an ugly grimace. "Three years later and I'm still hurting her. Funny, isn't it?"

"Mac... don't move. You'll cut yourself." She reached for the broom, empathy squeezing her heart.

"It was my fault," he said as though she hadn't spoken a word. "I was supposed to be driving her to our first prenatal ultrasound. Instead, I blew her off to get in an extra hour of practice—ironic, huh? Now I have nothing but time."

He bent and picked up the ruined frame, ignoring the shards of glass ready to rip his skin to shreds. "She didn't deserve to die that way. Neither one of them. It was a girl, you know—the baby." He glanced up at Sam, a wealth of pain shimmering in stormy gray eyes. "We were supposed to find out together—not like that. Never like that." He cradled the picture to his chest, shoulders hunched over the frame.

Sam set aside the broom to embrace the broad back that seemed so solid but hid a broken heart. Tears he wouldn't release slid down her chin and dampened his skin. It had been hard to lose her father, she couldn't imagine what he was going through. He'd probably bottled it all up inside until now. He had to understand it wasn't his fault, the accident probably would have happened whether he was there or not—panic flared—and then they would never have met.

Worried he'd cut himself if she didn't get the glass cleared away, Sam brushed the tears from her cheeks and carried on with the job of sweeping the shards into a dustpan. Once she had it picked up, she hurried to the den, flicked on the light and located the slippers she'd remembered near the sofa the night before. Cleo lay curled into the corner of the couch and peeked sleepily up at her before tucking her head back into her chest. Good. It was best if she stayed out of the kitchen until Sam had a chance to damp mop. It was pitch black outside beyond the still-open drapes. It gave her an eerie feeling, as though someone was staring in at her, so she took a moment to snap the curtains closed before racing back to Mac.

He'd risen and placed the photo on the island. He turned when she burst into the room and she gasped. The haggard look was bad enough, but he'd nicked his chest from the broken glass and had little rivulets of blood staining his skin.

"You're hurt." Sam went to the sink and dampened a cloth she found in a nearby drawer, then strode around the island and carefully cleaned the scratches. She grimaced at the particles embedded in the wounds. "These cuts need to be washed. I'm worried about infection." She felt Mac's gaze on her face and glanced up to see a strange look in his eyes. "What?" she muttered, suddenly uncomfortable in her own skin.

"Why do you care?" he asked, his head tipped to the side as though he was trying to figure her out. "Half the time I'm a rude bastard around you and yet you're still here, helping me."

"Only half?" she joked.

He covered her hand with his, holding it over his heart. "I'm serious, Sam. You can do better. Don't get hooked on me, I'm not worth it."

She pushed away, embarrassed, and returned to the sink to rinse the cloth. She laughed over the noise of running water. "You aren't that irresistible, Wanowski. Get over yourself." A stray glass sliver neatly sliced her palm—sort of like he'd just done to her heart—and she squeezed her fingers over it, hiding the cut until she could tend to it alone. She didn't think she could handle his touch right now.

The weight of his words hovered between them like an oppressive blanket until she was ready to scream, *"Leave already, just go."* But of course, she didn't, because that would mean she cared, and they both knew that would be a mistake.

"Are you okay?" he asked, his reflection in the window dripping regret.

"Sure. I'm fine. I'll see you in the morning." *Don't talk, please... just go.* Her throat was knotted so tight she could barely breathe, never mind act as though everything was fine.

Fine.

That was some word choice; as though they were talking about the weather or the price of gas.

"Nice day today."

"It's fine."

"Did you notice gas dropped a penny?"

"That's fine."

"I'm sorry for ripping your heart out."

"Sure, I'm fine."

After Mac's reflection shuffled out of the kitchen, Sam stared at the blood blending with the cool water in the palm of her hand and wondered if she'd ever be *fine* again.

———

MAC CASTIGATED himself all the way upstairs and into his cold, lonely room. He was a first-class idiot for hurting Sam the way he had. He'd known she wasn't a casual hook-up when they met, and yet he'd still taken her to bed. If only she didn't tempt him with those baby-blue eyes or luscious pink lips. He could still feel her silky blond hair pooling at his waist as she... shit, he needed to quit thinking about her or he'd be banging on her bedroom door and that would lead to complications he couldn't handle right now.

His priority had to be to his team.

Restless, he wandered over to the heavy oak dresser —part of a suite that gave the room a chalet feeling— and noticed his cell phone. Maybe if Sam's had service, his would too. Sure enough, he powered the high-tech gadget up and found a long list of incoming calls he'd missed, a good number of them from the coach, and a few texts from Samson.

HOW'S CABIN LIFE?

· · ·

I HEAR the new therapist is hot. Go, man, show her your hammer, lol

MAC FROWNED. The jackass. The next text raised his brows.

COACH IS ON THE WARPATH. *Stay out of his way. He's got it out for you.*

Now WHAT? He'd pushed himself past his limits during PT so he could get back to the game, what more did the guy want? He scrubbed a hand down his chest and winced as the cuts registered. *Sam.* The sooner they could get back to town and reality the better. He was in danger of believing the second chance fantasy, and that would be a mistake. He'd only break her heart.

He dialed the coach and waited.

"About time. You forget you're still employed, Wanowski? That could change." Harris's rusty voice grated in Mac's ear. He walked over to the bed and sat, abstractedly noticing it had been made sometime during the day. Sam again. Her touch was everywhere.

"It's not like I'm holidaying, Coach. You sent me here, remember?" Five years and Mac could count on one hand how many times he'd seen Coach Harris smile, and never at him. But the man knew how to take a team to the top—that was about his only saving grace.

"Yeah, yeah, can the excuses. Doc tells me he drove Samantha Walters up there to be your therapist. I don't know what the hell Thomas was thinking, leaving her alone with the likes of you. You'd better have been treating her with respect, Sam's special."

Mac stiffened. "I haven't taken to eating little girls for breakfast, yet," he said. "She's not my type. Don't worry about it."

He caught a soft gasp and looked up just as the bedroom door slid shut on a whisper. *Sam.* He'd forgotten to close the door earlier and now he'd done the one thing he'd swore he never would—he'd hurt her.

He started to rise and go after her, then sighed and sank back down. Maybe this was for the best. They never would have worked anyway. Too bad his heart didn't agree.

He lifted the phone to his ear. "Come get us. I'm ready to play hockey."

17

Sᴀᴍ ᴄᴏᴜʟᴅɴ'ᴛ sʟᴇᴇᴘ after overhearing Mac on the phone. At first, she'd been incredibly hurt but a little snuggle-time on the sofa with Cleo helped her come to the realization Mac was trying to protect her. He liked to think he was the big, tough hockey player, but inside, he had a marshmallow heart. She'd seen the evidence of that herself last night with his wife's photo. And what about the cat? How many guys kept their wife's pet long after she was gone? Maybe he wasn't ready for a relationship yet—she could understand that—but there had to be a way to convince him to give love another chance, even if it turned out not to be with her. Though the thought of Mac with another woman was a stab to the heart.

She curled her toes into the cushions and lightly massaged Cleo's soft belly, smiling at how the resultant purr sounded like a car not firing on all cylinders. Crazy how fast she'd come to care for a man she'd met for the first time barely two weeks ago. The cabin in the woods had become a haven—their place. She might not get another chance; when they returned to the city life would resume its frenetic pace. They each had obligations that would be like a wedge driving them apart. Did she really want to waste this night?

Cleo's ears perked and she lifted her head to stare at the doorway. Sam's pulse took flight, zinging through her veins at rocket speed. Mac leaned against the doorframe, still wearing those faded blue jeans, except now the button was undone, as though he'd been getting ready for bed. Her breath hitched and she placed a hand to her throat. He could pose for a GQ magazine cover, he was that gorgeous.

"Hey," he said, the low timbre of his voice tightening her nipples. "What are you doing down here?"

Cleo expressed her disapproval by digging in her claws and hopping down to glide from the room, nose in the air.

"Ow," Sam muttered and rubbed at her leg. "That cat has a temper."

Mac chuckled and straightened to stroll to the club chair across from her. "Mind if I join you?"

Did she? Now that he was here, all her earlier bravado faded, and the insecurities rolled in. "Are you sure you want to? I thought we said everything that needed to be said—or *you* did, anyway."

He hesitated, but eventually sank into the deep chair with a sigh. "Sam, I don't want it to end like this. I care about you—" she snorted, "—and hope we can remain friends."

Friends. *Ouch*. He'd just sounded the death knell on her plans to woo him until dawn's early light.

"Do you say that to all the girls?" she asked and didn't much care if it sounded waspish. "I'm curious how many buy that line." On the outside she looked cool and calm—she hoped—while inside her dreams shattered like the glass from the picture frame.

Mac's brow rose and his lips quirked into a near smile—the jerk. "All my girls, huh?" He leaned forward and unclenched her fist so that he could inspect the cut on her palm. "Why didn't you tell me you cut yourself?"

Sam jerked. The sensation of his calloused fingertip tracing a line on her skin created exquisite chills to skate up and down her spine. "It's nothing. Can I have my hand back, please?" Before she embarrassed herself by moaning.

Mac glanced up, the concerned expression in his eyes morphing into something much more predatory. "Are you sure?" he murmured, and they both knew he wasn't talking about her fingers. He lifted her hand, his lips whispering a kiss across her palm. "We're good together, Sam."

Yes, they were. But, what about when tomorrow arrived? She didn't do casual hookups, and it was beginning to sound as though that's all Mac was interested in.

She was tempted though. So tempted.

That kind of thinking led to heartbreak.

Regretfully, she disengaged her hand from his and folded hers onto her lap, fingers closing over her palm to hold the warmth from his mouth. "I don't think that's a good idea. We had fun—let's leave it like that, okay?"

Mac's eyes narrowed, and for one breath-stealing moment she thought he was going to fight for her, but then he shrugged and settled into the chair, the hands she wanted all over her body curled over the armrests.

"Who are you trying to convince?" he asked. "You're damn good at sending out mixed messages."

"Me?" she squeaked. Outrage took care of any lingering regrets. "You're the one coming on to me after telling whoever it was on the phone that, and I quote, "*she's not my type.*" You could have fooled me, or do you bed every female you meet, type or no type?" Unable to sit that close to him for another second without doing something drastic, like clouting him over the head with the lamp, Sam rose and strode across the room to the bay window. She swept the curtain aside and stared out at the pitch-dark night. She was a masochist. What other explanation could there be for continually falling under this man's spell?

She sensed Mac before his hands gripped her shoulders and turned her to face him.

"What do you say to starting over?" He tipped her chin up so he could see her eyes. "We seem to have gotten off on a wrong foot tonight. What do you say, friends?"

Sam lowered her gaze to his chest and stared at the scratches—evidence of his fidelity. They may have made love, but his heart remained loyal to his wife. It was over. She couldn't compete with a ghost.

"Sure. Friends."

18

DAN KEPT one eye on the snow-covered road and the other on Doc sitting uncharacteristically silent in the passenger seat. They were both under a pile of stress at work, but this seemed different. More ominous.

"Okay, spit it out," he said, tired of his own company. "What's wrong?" He frowned at the dark line of clouds building on the horizon and stepped a bit harder on the gas pedal. The snowbanks were window high on either side of his SUV, closing them in on the narrow country road. He hated winter driving, but Thomas thought his vehicle wouldn't make it so here he was, ploughing through bloody drifts for a hockey player he couldn't stand. *Ain't life grand.*

Thomas jerked as though he'd been deep in thought. He reached over and tried to turn up the heat, but it was already set on high. "Your heater is broken," he grumbled.

Dan sighed. He shouldn't be surprised, he'd known the day was going to suck before they left town. "There's a throw in the backseat if you're cold. You want to tell me why you're giving me the silent treatment?"

Doc turned the vents to aim his way before glancing over. "Sorry. I have a lot on my mind. Appreciate you driving today. Samantha will be happy to see you."

Dan wanted to see her, too, and make sure those idiots he'd hired to scare off Wanowski hadn't done anything to hurt a hair on his goddaughter's head. "I still can't believe she's up here. You should have run it by me first, Thomas, you know that." He hated when his authority was questioned—probably one of the main reasons Wanowski rubbed him wrong. The WarHawks' captain seemed to take pleasure in challenging him at every turn.

But, not for much longer.

"He's *my* patient, Coach. It's my responsibility to get him rehabilitated and back to work. I was doing my job." Doc's tone was frosty.

Dan frowned. He couldn't remember a time his old friend had been so abrupt. Normally, Thomas was the antithesis of grumpy old man. The team players completely entrusted themselves into his care and he'd never let them down. He and Doc went back a long way—twenty years. It bothered him to have this rift between them.

"Look man, what's done is done. As long as Sam is okay, and Wanowski is ready to win us the cup, what do you say we forget it? No harm, no foul."

The tires lost traction for an instant and Doc straightened in his seat. "Slow down before you get us killed."

Dan bit back the expletive hovering on the edge of his tongue. Bickering their way up the mountain wouldn't do anything to ease the growing strain. He slowed down and moved over for the plow going the other way. There was a brief moment of total whiteout conditions, thanks to the spray created by the big truck. When they burst through the other side, he heaved a giant sigh and released his death grip on the steering wheel. "Whew, that was a close one."

"Maybe, I should have driven," Doc said, his hand locked around the holy-shit handle.

Dan looked over and grinned. "Too much excitement for you, old-timer?"

Thomas scowled and dropped his arm. He took a long swallow from a go-cup filled with hot coffee mixed with milk and sugar—too much sugar, so far as Dan was concerned. "Now I remember why I moved to

Victoria, to get away from this crap," he said, and wiped a slightly shaky hand across his mouth.

Amen to that. Dan didn't know why anyone would choose to isolate themselves in the back of beyond the way Donaldson had with this cabin. Most of the players invested in swanky condos or million-dollar homes in the city. But it had worked to get Wanowski out of his way long enough to create the conjecture amongst the fans needed before the playoffs. Now, when they entered the arena, it would be as the underdog—right where he wanted them.

Doc pointed to a break in the trees, showing a nearly invisible road on the right. "That's it there. About five miles straight up."

Oh, joy. Dan signaled—though, who was going to care, the deer?—and slowed for the turn. It immediately became apparent the road was little more than a goat path and hadn't been plowed in some time. Between the evergreens towering over them and the colorless landscape, it was easy to feel small and insignificant. It made him antsy.

"They'd better be ready to go. I'm not hanging around out here all damn day," he grumbled, sneaking another glance at the mushrooming gray clouds. "That storm is going to hit sooner rather than later."

Doc nodded. "Sam promised she'd have everything

ready to go. We should be back to town in time for dinner."

Dan's stomach chose that moment to rumble. Small wonder, they'd left at the butt crack of dawn this morning. He'd had to settle for a six-pack of donuts with his coffee and had finished both before they'd even left the highway. "Good, I think I'll make Wanowski buy us a steak for being such a giant pain in the ass."

Thomas chuckled. "I have a feeling he thinks the same about you."

The SUV crept slowly up the hill, now and then bouncing over washboards hidden under the snow. The clock on the dash read two pm, but it seemed closer to evening with the overcast skies. They hadn't seen another soul since the plow truck, which made Dan wonder where Hewett and his partner were holed up. There weren't a lot of homes in the area, though if they were mercenaries like they purported themselves to be, he guessed they could find a cave or whatever outdoorsy people did in storms. As long as they stayed out of sight, he didn't give a shit. They hadn't been worth the money he had to fork over, that's for sure. He could have done a better job himself.

"There it is," Doc announced as the house rose out of the gloom.

Dan had to give Donaldson credit, the place looked nicer than he'd expected—smaller, too. No way was he getting stuck up here with Wanowski in a blizzard. Fate couldn't be that unkind. Of course, that's when the snow decided to fall. Big, fat flakes that covered the windshield like decoupage. He flicked on the wipers and took grim satisfaction in destroying Mother Nature's artwork.

"About damn time," he said as he pulled up in front of an impressive set of stairs leading to a wrap-around deck. "Well, where are they then?" He tapped the horn impatiently.

Thomas shot him a disgusted look. "Give them a second to get to the door, why don't you?" He opened the car door and let in a gust of cold air. "Besides, I need to use the facilities before we leave." He grunted as he climbed out of the vehicle and stretched, then frowned when Dan remained where he was. "You plan on staying here by yourself?" He shook his head and slammed the door shut.

Dan watched as Doc climbed the stairs and knocked on the door to the house. He could either sit here shivering or go in and get them all moving himself. The door opened and warm interior light spilled onto the deck. Fine, he'd go in and make nice, then. Damn, Wanowski.

19

Mac opened the door to Doc and stood back to let him in, a mixture of relief and regret churning in his gut. The time on Mount Washington with Sam had turned out to be so much more than he'd expected. *She* was more than he'd expected.

"Good to see you, Doc. Look, no crutches." Mac tipped his leg one way, then the other, pleased with the returning mobility. "Come on in, it's chilly out there." He moved aside so the other man could enter but froze when the coach's ruddy face appeared as he climbed the stairs to the deck. "I see you've brought company."

"Play nice," Doc warned. "Now where's that niece of mine? I need a hug."

"I'm here, Uncle. I've missed you." Sam stepped into the hall and hurried into his arms. They were almost the same height and shared a strong family resemblance with the honey blond hair—though Doc's was more white than blond—and cornflower blue eyes.

"Has this young man been treating you right?" Doc patted her shoulder and peered into her face. "If not, I have connections. We can make him disappear." His smile was a trifle too enigmatic for Mac's comfort.

He nodded to the coach as he entered and was pretty sure the chill that followed him in wasn't all weather related. "Coach. I wasn't expecting to see you out here. How's the team?"

"Good, no thanks to you." Coach Harris shivered violently, then proceeded to cough up a lung. When he got his breath back, he opened his arms to Sam. "Got a hug for the old man?" he asked, his voice raspy.

Sam sent an apologetic glance toward Mac before leaning in to give the coach a peck on the cheek. "Thank you for keeping Uncle Thomas company, Uncle Dan. Though it sounds like you'd be better off in bed."

Uncle Dan? The coach was Sam's uncle, too? What the hell? Was this some kind of twisted game they were playing? Screw with the hockey player's head until he quit. He could see the coach coming up with something like that—but the joke was on him. Mac had slept with the decoy.

Anger propelled him down the hall. He needed a few minutes to get his head on straight, before he said something he'd regret. He could hear their laughter even after he closed himself into the den, and it seemed to mock everything he'd come to feel for Sam. Could she really have been a party to a collusion of this magnitude? He didn't want to believe it, but what other explanation could there be? It was common knowledge the coach couldn't stand him. If the doc and Sam were related to him somehow, then it followed they wouldn't have his best interests at heart. He'd been a fool.

"Hey," Sam said from behind him. "We wondered where you'd gone. Is anything wrong?"

Mac turned and barely refrained from snarling. She looked like a dream come true, standing there. The light streaming in over his shoulder created a halo, her beauty ethereal in the soft rays of the sun. So lovely; a seductress sent to destroy him—and she'd almost succeeded.

"Some family you have there. No wonder you managed to get a contract with the team on your credentials." His hands clenched at his sides. It was either that or give in to the urge to wrap them around her scheming throat. She looked puzzled, then increasingly angry. Maybe he should add actress to her qualifications.

She stepped into the room and carefully shut the door before rounding on him, her chin thrust out like a pugilist's. "I don't know what crawled up your butt, Wanowski, but you can just take those mean words and, and... shove them."

He smirked, though the situation was anything except funny. "That's the best you can come up with? You better grow a thicker skin than that if you plan on playing with the big boys." He swung over to the bar fridge and cracked open a beer, though the frothy stuff caught in his throat. "How long were you and the coach planning to keep me from playing? Did he send you out here to *distract* me, Sam? Keep the big, dumb hockey player busy, right?" He took another drink, then laughed. "Well, sugar, you certainly did a fine job. I wasn't thinking of the puck last night while we messed up your sheets, that's for damn sure. Your *uncle* should give you a raise."

A sharp gasp echoed from behind and the next second a hand reached over his arm and upended the bottle of beer down his shirtfront. "No wonder Uncle Thomas was hesitant about bringing me out here, you're just as big a jerk as everyone says you are."

Mac grimaced as the beer forged a trail down his chest and under the waistband of his jeans. *Damn, that was cold.*

Sam stared at him. "Where is this coming from, Mac? I thought we were past your attitude—that we'd made a connection."

He didn't trust the betrayal in her gaze. "Why didn't you tell me the coach was your uncle? Don't you think that's something I should have known?" He fisted the shirt at his back and tugged it over his head, then used the soft cotton to dry his stomach. "Damn, I smell like a brewery now." He glanced up and caught her biting her plump lower lip, her eyes tracking his hands. His pulse kicked in response. He turned away and threw the discarded shirt on a chair before he did what his body was urging and took her in his arms. "Quit looking at me that way," he said, his voice little more than gravel scaping his throat.

She glared. "Quit stripping in front of me, then." She crossed her arms over her chest and glanced over her shoulder—looking for reinforcements, maybe? "He's not my uncle." Her gaze met his, then flitted away. "Dan Harris is my godfather. He's known our family for years. I didn't think it was relevant because Uncle Thomas hired me, it had nothing to do with Uncle Dan." Her eyes came back to his, pleading. "Please, Mac. You have to believe me."

Did he? It was possible Doc had overstepped his bounds, but Mac still smelled a subterfuge. He'd learned to trust his gut out on the ice, and it was telling him there was something going on here—he just had to figure out whether Sam was a part of it.

Sam didn't know what had triggered Mac's sudden mistrust, but it hurt. Even though they'd—he'd—decided to keep their relationship casual, she'd mistakenly thought he cared about her. Now she wasn't so sure. His anger at her godfather seemed deeply personal. She couldn't understand how the jovial man she'd grown up with could incite that kind of suspicion.

She glanced at the closed door. Her uncles had gone to the kitchen to make sandwiches for the road, but soon they'd be wondering where she and Mac were, and she didn't want them finding out about his outburst. Though why she should want to protect him after the things he'd accused her of doing... He'd actually believed she would sleep with him in order to keep her job. So much for thinking they had something special. Then again, he'd been looking for ways to distance himself from their relationship since it began. Guess he'd found it.

"Are you going to tell them what I said?" Mac asked, following her gaze to the door.

Seriously? He had so little confidence in her, he thought she'd go running straight to her uncles? Fine. She was done with this conversation—maybe even with Mac.

She straightened her spine and strode for the door.

"No. I wouldn't want them to think I'm hurt because you used me like one of those hockey bunnies. You're not worth it. Goodbye, Mac."

"Sam, wait," he said to her back as she swung the door open. Coach stood on the other side, a chagrined look on his grizzled face.

"Uncle..." she started, but when she noticed the black pistol pointed at his back, her mind went blank.

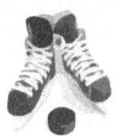

20

SAM COULDN'T COMPREHEND what she was seeing. Her beloved Uncle Thomas held a menacing gun in a shaky two-handed grip, his pale face set in stone.

"Move," he told Uncle Dan, nudging him into the room with the muzzle of the weapon. "I don't want to hurt you—any of you—but I will, if necessary."

"I... I don't understand," she whispered, her skin going clammy.

"It's pretty simple," Mac drawled, startling her into glancing his way. He gave a slight jerk of his head to the right and she realized he wanted her to join him. "Your uncle found out how big an asshole the coach is and decided to do something about it. Right, Doc?"

"Takes one to know one, Wanowski," Coach muttered.

"Shut up," Uncle Thomas snarled and gave Dan a shove. "Sit down, all of you." He hesitated, something like remorse sifting through his eyes as he nodded at Sam. "You too, my dear." He waited while Dan shuffled into a nearby club chair and Sam perched on the edge of the sofa. When Mac remained at the bar, he turned the gun on him. "I'm not playing games, Mac. I said *sit* down."

Glass shattered as a shot blasted through the room. Sam screamed and covered her ears. Shocked, she stared at the blood blooming on Mac's arm. "What have you done?" she cried, sending her uncle a horrified glance. She jumped to her feet and hurried to Mac's side, ignoring her uncle's bark to stay where she was. "Mac, god, I'm so sorry." She tried to get a look at the injury, but he pushed her away, angling his body between her and Thomas.

"It's fine, just a scratch. You shouldn't be here," he said, his gaze on Doc as he used his left hand to staunch the wound. He raised his voice, "You hear me, you crazy old man? Let Sam go. For Christ's sake, she's your niece. What do you hope to accomplish by holding us like this?"

Uncle Thomas frowned. "I don't want to hurt anyone," he repeated. "If you do as I say, this will be over before you know it." He muttered something under his breath that Sam couldn't understand, then strode to the window and glanced out, keeping to the side so he could stay out of sight and maintain an eye on the room.

Sam reached for the clean white towel folded on the edge of the sink, careful to let her uncle see what she was doing. "Let me see that arm," she said quietly. Her stomach rolled at the sight of the blood seeping between Mac's fingers. She might be a therapist with first aid training, but gunshot wounds were out of her wheelhouse.

"I think it's from the glass." He craned his head to see the ugly gash. "Guess you were right. If I'd kept my shirt on, it probably would have barely grazed me." He nudged her with his good arm. "Aren't you going to say, "*I told you so?*""

"Mac, this isn't funny," she whispered, on the verge of tears. She dabbed at the edges of the gaping four-inch slash, relieved that she wasn't looking at a round bullet hole. Either her uncle had meant to miss, or he wasn't a good shot. Hopefully, he'd have no more reasons to prove it, one way or the other.

"Believe me, I'm not laughing." Mac gently took the towel and wiped his hand clean as best he could. "Want to tell me what's going on?" He kept a close watch on Doc's movements, and Sam prayed he wasn't thinking of doing something stupid—like getting himself killed.

"How can you ask me that?" Reaction was setting in, that must be why she couldn't stop her teeth from chattering or the thick taste of betrayal from coating her throat. Her uncle's duplicity was bad enough, but that Mac assumed she might be a part of it...? That hurt.

"Well, I find it suspicious that all of my problems started with you. I've been shot at, knocked unconscious, almost burned alive, and now held at gunpoint. You take high maintenance to a whole new level, babe."

Grr. Sam was tempted to shoot him herself. She had a feeling he was trying to distract her from the very real danger they were in, but their time would be better spent finding a way out of this mess. Her uncle couldn't be in his right mind, he was acting totally out of character. Maybe he'd sustained some sort of psychotic episode? If she could talk him out of whatever crazy plan he'd concocted, they could get him help.

But first, he had to put *down* that gun.

"Uncle Thomas, please. Mom wouldn't want you to be doing this. Can't we just talk? Maybe there's something we can do." She took a step toward him, only to be brought up short by Mac's hand on her shoulder. She glared at him and tried to break free, but his grip only tightened. Giving up, she returned her attention to her uncle. He'd gone back to sneaking gazes out the window, for all the world acting as though they were under attack.

"That idiot's gone off the deep end. There's no talking to him," Coach said, his expression disgusted more than frightened. "I knew coming up here was a mistake."

Doc frowned at his old friend. "It's time to come clean, Dan. I know what you've done."

Sam felt like Alice falling down the rabbit hole, Mac's hold on her arm the only anchor in a topsy-turvy world. None of this made any sense. Her beloved family had become strangers. Frustrated, she fisted her hair in both hands and took a deep breath. She released her grip and let her hands fall. "*What* is going on?"

"Sam, calm down. It's going to be okay." Mac tugged her back, against his chest, and wrapped comforting arms around her waist. "Trust me," he whispered.

More than anything, she wanted to lean into his strength and soak it up as her own, but she forced herself to stand straight. This was her problem, not his. Thomas and Dan had continued their bickering and when she picked up on the conversation it was to hear the coach admitting to complicity in the fire from last week.

"Those idiots. They were supposed to disarm the truck so *he—*" Dan pointed at Mac, "—stayed put." His gaze sharpened on Doc. "It's you. You're the one behind this, aren't you?" He shook his head and laughed. "I'm such a fool. Here I thought I was in the mob's pocket for gambling, but it was you the whole time."

Mac's arms had gradually tightened until her ribs hurt from the pressure. "Are you telling me you *hired* those goons that shot at us?"

She gasped, suddenly grateful for his hold as her legs turned weak. "Uncle?" Her vision wavered. She could have died. Mac had been hurt and her own family was behind it. She slumped. Through a fog she could hear Mac calling her name, and then his hand pushing her head between her knees.

"Breathe, honey. Just breathe." He brushed her hair away from her face with a gentle hand. "Get her some water."

Sam stared at her shoes, absently noting the scuff on the toe. She'd have to polish them when she got home. They'd been a foolish luxury last Christmas, a treat after passing her courses and getting her degree. The degree she'd received thanks to her uncle.

Oh, my God.

She stiffened and lifted her head to stare at the man who'd paid for her education, her brother's schooling, and her mother's house. "It's my fault," she whispered and saw the truth in his blue eyes, so like her own. "You did this for us."

[21]

MAC ACCEPTED the water glass from Coach Harris. Animosity aside, they needed to become allies if there was any hope of putting an end to this nightmare. He slid a sideways glance at Sam's uncle, then met Coach's gaze. A slight dip of the head and the play was in motion for the most important game of their careers—protecting Sam.

"You should have told us," Sam said, her voice regaining its strength. "We could have worked it out. Where did the money come from, Uncle Thomas?"

Mac was relieved to see the color returning to her translucent skin. He couldn't imagine what she was going through. His gut roiled at the betrayal and he wasn't related to the old codgers. If he could just get that gun away from Doc... Coach had moved to the other side of the room, clearly waiting for his chance to end this thing, as well.

"Here, drink this." Mac handed the water to Sam. His brows lowered at the chill in her fingers. He nodded toward the fireplace. "Mind if I start a fire? She's frozen."

Doc hesitated then waved the firearm at the hearth. "No funny stuff, Hammer. I know your tricks." He turned to Sam. "I suppose I owe you an explanation." He took a seat on the window bench and rubbed his neck, the hand holding the gun at rest on his thigh. "You have to understand; your mom and I had a... less than optimal childhood. I don't know if she ever spoke of our father to you kids, but let's just say, he had a temper."

Mac gathered some kindling, grimacing at the stiffness in his injured arm, and got the fire started while keeping an eye on Sam. How was she going to handle her uncle airing the family skeletons? "Is this necessary?" he asked. What benefit could there be in telling her about dark family secrets?

Thomas's hairy gray beetle brows met over his prominent nose. "Is this too hard for you, dear?"

How could he talk so sweet while holding a gun on them? Mac used the poker to shift the embers around and added a couple of good-sized logs over the spray of sparks. The heat singed his skin and he yanked his hand back, narrowly missing the handle to the damper. *The flue.* He could use that.

"It's okay, Mac. I want to hear this." Sam took a small sip of water and set the glass on the coffee table. "My grandfather died before we were born. I thought Mom missed him, she never talked about him."

Thomas stared at the floor, lost in thought. "Your mom was the best big sister anyone could wish for. She often protected me when Father came home smelling of liquor. Sometimes...," he rubbed his forehead, "sometimes she took the punishments in my place." His eyes were moist when he lifted his head. "I would do anything for your mother, you have to know that."

Coach snorted. "This sob story is great, but it doesn't explain how you could swindle your best friend—me."

Mac's throat ached. These admissions were ripping Sam's heart to shreds. They hadn't known each other long, but the fact that family was important to her radiated from her pores. His parents had been too busy conquering the world to have time for a small boy. They'd foisted him off on friends and cousins for most of his childhood. The first real home he'd known came with his marriage to Jess. The pang her name conjured was more bittersweet than gut-wrenching this time, as though she supported his burgeoning feelings for Sam. He'd like to believe that, anyway.

"I didn't *swindle* you, as you put it." Doc's spine went rigid. "Your gambling issues are your own, I just provided the means, that's all."

"How, Uncle Thomas? How did you help any of us?" Sam leaned forward in her seat, her gaze intense. "I should have realized something was wrong. A doctor doesn't make the kind of money you gave to us. What did you do?" She wrung her hands together.

"What I had to do," Doc said, his gaze pleading with her to understand. "I met some business men. They offered me a deal and I accepted. It was only supposed to be temporary, just while the twenty-seven-teen playoffs were on, but when they asked me to do things I didn't agree with, accidents began to happen." His gaze slid to Mac and away again. "I had no choice. And after that, they had me over a barrel. It's gone on since then; gambling, money laundering, drugs, what-ever they demanded of me I was forced to do, or they threatened to hurt my family." He hung his head. "I had no choice."

Three years ago. Accidents. A sick feeling twisted Mac's stomach in knots. Could it be? He rose and started across the room, heedless of the loaded gun. "You caused Jess's death?" His hands fisted. "You dirty son-of-a..."

"Mac," Sam cried, just as Doc lifted the pistol.

"That's far enough," he ordered. "If you force me to shoot again, I won't miss this time."

"You're going to pay, old man. If it's the last thing I do, my wife and daughter *will* get justice." Mac ached to wring Doc's neck, but Sam needed him. He had to think with his head and not his heart. He returned to his stance in front of the fireplace, and on the pretense of stirring the flames, closed the damper.

DAN WATCHED the circus that was going on and thanked the Lord he had no family of his own. They were too much trouble. The only person he was accountable to was himself—and he liked it that way. At first, he'd been furious with Thomas for pulling the wool over his eyes but had to admire a man with the cojones to do what he had for those he loved. Too bad it was going to end up costing him his life. If it came down to a choice between Dan's neck and his old buddy's... well, there really was no choice.

Wanowski, the hot-headed idiot, stomped over to the fireplace and stirred up the embers. Sparks exploded in flashes of red and orange and as the flames hissed, he nonchalantly pressed the handle on the damper, thereby closing the flue. Okay, not so dumb. In five or ten minutes this room would fill with noxious gas and they'd all be choking like a bunch of potheads from the fumes. That would be his chance to get the hell out of here—let those two fight it out and he'd be there to pick up the pieces.

"Uncle Thomas, if you would just go to the police, they could help you." Sam gazed at Mac's tensed back, the love in her eyes apparent to everyone else in the room, before refocusing on her uncle. "I refuse to believe you deliberately set out to... to injure Mac's family. Tell the police what happened, and it'll all work out, you'll see."

Mac swore and swung around, his gaze furious. "You want me to let you brush this under the carpet as though it were a minor infraction? *No*. Have you ever seen the wreck of a vehicle from a side collision?" He punched one closed fist into his open hand, and they all flinched. "There was nothing left of the driver's side from the force of the impact. They had to use the jaws of life to pry her from that mangled mess. She was dead before they got her to the hospital—before I could say goodbye." He wiped his eyes with his bare forearm and stared Sam down. "No. Not even for you. He has to pay." He coughed and moved away from the fireplace, closer to Sam. "I'm sorry. Really, I am."

Dan's eyes began to burn. He knew it was the fumes but had to admit Wanowski's story got to him. No wonder the guy was touchy. He'd heard of the accident, of course—the team had attended the funeral, but the details were kept hush-hush to avoid a media frenzy. At the time he'd just signed on as head coach to the WarHawks and had his hands full learning the ropes. He'd made the mistake of using a bookie to bet on a few games and soon became well and truly bitten by the gambling bug. The same insect who'd destroyed Doc's life—and by association, Wanowski's—apparently. For a moment, he toyed with the idea of joining forces with Thomas, going to the cops, and bringing the mob kingpin down—whoever he was. But then reality set in. Turn on the mob and you better have eyes in the back of your head, otherwise they'd be fitting you out with a pair of cement shoes. No, it was time for him and his old friend to part ways, though he was sorry Sam was caught in the middle. Maybe, he'd send her some dough after his next win—anonymously, of course.

The room grew hazy, just a hint at first, but then more obvious as the smoke built up in the hearth and seeped into the den. Sam felt the effects first, bowing over and coughing until she could barely draw breath. Mac and Dan joined in—Dan's lungs on fire. Doc, being furthest away, was the last to succumb, but he was also the oldest and not as fit as the rest. His face turned red as he strove to breathe past the harsh coughs ripping at his lungs. He set the gun down and wrapped his arms around his chest, bending over to gasp like a fish out of water.

Dan rose and stumbled toward the door, partly to gain fresh air, but mostly to bolt while he could. By now the smoke was so thick, he doubted anyone even saw him escape into the hall, but just to be sure he closed the door and braced a chair under the knob. There, that should keep them busy for a while. Now, to get out of this hellhole.

He hurried down the hall and gave a sigh of relief as he stepped outside. One that was short-lived.

"Dan Harris, RCMP. Put your hands in the air. You are under arrest." Four officers, their dark hats ringed with yellow bands, stepped out of the twilight and converged on the house, weapons drawn.

"You can't arrest me," Dan sputtered. "On what charge?" He was all bravado on the outside. Inside, his heart had fallen to his shoes.

A young officer, barely out of high school by the look of him, took his hands and yanked them behind his back while reading him his rights. The cold steel of handcuffs bit his wrists and his mouth dried. "I want a lawyer."

"You will have the opportunity to call a lawyer or have one appointed for you. Do you understand, Mr. Harris?" Another officer stared him in the eye. "This isn't a game, sir. You are in serious trouble, as is your associate, Mr. Thomas Edwards. Where is Mr. Edwards?"

Faking a bluster he didn't feel, Dan snarled, "I don't know. Do you know who you're talking to? I'm head coach of the NHL's Victoria WarHawks. I'm here with the team's medic to check on our captain, Mac Wanowski. What could possibly be wrong with that?"

The cop didn't even blink. "We asked you a question, sir. Make things easy on yourself. Tell us what we need to know."

"Suit yourself, he's in there." Dan jerked his chin over his shoulder.

The cop doing the grilling nodded to the silent two and they disappeared around the side of the house. He lifted his gun even with his shoulder, muzzle pointed at the sky and waited while the young cop shuffled Dan down the stairs toward the waiting patrol cars.

Dan glanced back in time to see the officer breach the front door. His stomach churned. "You never said, what are you arresting me for?"

A hand pressed down on his head, guiding him into the back of the car. "Organized crime. You're being charged with racketeering, sir."

22

SAM'S CHEST heaved with the effort to draw a clean breath as a deadly haze filled the den. *Dear Lord, was the house on fire now?* She peered through streaming eyes, heart beating against her ribs like a trapped animal as grunts erupted from across the room. She gasped. Mac and her uncle were fighting for control of the gun. While Mac was undoubtedly younger and stronger, Uncle Thomas was agile and had a firm grip on the weapon as it dipped between their bodies. Someone was going to get killed.

"Uncle Dan, help," she cried, choking on the fumes. She glanced around desperately, but the coach was gone. Not knowing what else to do, Sam hefted the heavy iron poker over her shoulder and lurched across the room. "Stop it. Uncle Thomas, please," she sobbed.

If he pressed the trigger... She couldn't bear to think of it.

The two men twirled in a deadly dance. She panicked, bringing the makeshift club down on her uncle's back as he bent over, battling to keep possession of the revolver. He roared and let go, his body bowing backward in a rictus of pain. He sank to his knees, groaning and coughing in equal measure. Mac backed away, the gun aimed at Doc's head, his face a forbidding mask. Sam dropped to her uncle's side and wrapped her arms carefully around his neck as she gazed miserably at Mac. "He's hurt, can't you see that? Leave him alone."

Mac brushed a forearm over his eyes and coughed. "We need to get out of here. Can I trust you to watch him for a minute?"

Hadn't she just proven he could trust her? She'd chosen to land a blow on her own flesh and blood rather than the man she... cared about. Though, after today's revelations, it was a wonder he wasn't pointing that weapon at both of them. He must hate her family.

"Of course," she said quietly, then remembered the coach. "Be careful. I don't know where Uncle Dan is." There was no way she could make up for his wife's death, but it didn't stop her from hoping he could forgive her one day.

He hesitated, then held out a hand to help her up.

Thomas remained hunched against the wall, his eyes red and streaming. "I want you over here, where he can't reach you." Mac attempted to hand her the gun and when she flinched away, he forced it into her hand. "Take it. Have you used a gun before?"

Sam's stomach swirled sickeningly. "Ye... yes, a long time ago." Her father had taken the family to the gun range for the day, but she hadn't enjoyed herself then and she sure as heck wasn't now.

"Just keep him still, until I get that damper open. Good of the coach to stick around and help," he added sarcastically, bending to pick up the discarded poker. "Nice work, by the way."

Nice. What could be nice about attacking your own uncle with a steel bar? "Just hurry," she muttered. The gun felt like it weighed fifty pounds, her arms shook with the strain of holding it pointed in her uncle's direction.

Mac nodded, cleared his throat, and strode through the smoke, parting it like a curtain. Sam kept a worried gaze on her uncle. Her lungs hurt from the gases floating around the room, but he was pale and sweating. His left arm hung limply by his side. She had no reason to have empathy after the things he'd done, but...

"Uncle, are you all right?" she asked.

He lifted his head and she was shocked by how

frail he appeared. "I messed up good, didn't I?" He attempted a smile, but his lips didn't cooperate. "I'm sorry, sweetheart."

He was slurring. Sam's medical training kicked in. She raced to his side, set the gun on the bench, and searched his face. Blurry eyes, sagging mouth, loss of balance—her uncle was having a stroke.

"Mac, Mac help," she yelled. "Hang on, Uncle, don't worry, okay?" She was worried enough for both of them.

"What?" Mac asked, appearing by her side. At least the smoke seemed a bit lighter—a small blessing.

Just having him nearby gave Sam a needed boost of confidence. "Quick, we need aspirin. My uncle is having a stroke."

Mac frowned and glanced from her to his enemy, but her desperation must have got through to him. He turned toward the bar. "I think I saw a bottle on the shelf, hang on."

Sam squeezed her uncle's hand, concerned about the clamminess. "Do you have your cell phone?" she called over her shoulder.

"I tried while looking for the pills," he answered, handing her two from the bottle in his hand. "Still no signal." He waited until she managed to get the pills between Uncle Thomas's lips with a small drink of water. "I'm going to find the coach. Maybe his cell reception is better."

Her first reaction was, 'No, don't leave' but it was the right decision. "Okay, sure, but hurry. Thank you, Mac."

He surprised her with a quick, hard kiss on the lips. "Stay safe, you hear me?" he whispered, and then he was gone.

She pressed her fingers to her mouth and blinked back tears. Mac Wanowski was a good man—and she loved him.

The door rattled across the room and Mac cursed. "It's locked. I can't get out." He kicked the wooden panels, but they held strong. "Damn it, Harris. Open this door."

Sam's stomach dropped. She hugged her uncle. What were they going to do?

———

MAC RATTLED the knob and put a shoulder to the door, but nothing he tried would budge the sealed entry. What did Coach hope to achieve with this stunt? He glanced back; Sam's gaze was encouraging, as though she thought he could perform a miracle and save the man behind his wife's death. Funny thing was, he wanted to be Sam's hero. They could worry about the penalty Doc must pay after he received medical attention.

He could break the bay window if he had to but would rather find another way.

"Mac, hurry," Sam yelled.

Grimacing over the wrench in his knee from kicking the door, Mac took a couple steps back, then rushed it, throwing all his weight at the wooden panels. They cracked but didn't give. Again. And once more. Whatever held the door in place wasn't willing to budge.

He was failing her.

He dropped his forehead to the warm oak and closed his eyes. His heart was pulled in two directions. He ached to get retribution for his wife and yet... there was Sam.

He turned and watched her gently rub her uncle's shoulder. Whatever he had done, he was still her family and had earned her loyalty. Mac couldn't forget that.

He picked up the iron poker and started to cross the room. "We'll have to go through the window. Move back, Sam, and I'll help Doc."

She stared at him with wide eyes. "But it must be an eight foot drop. How are we going to get him out?"

"One problem at a time, okay?" He gave her a hand up and then obeyed the impulse to pull her close. She smelled of smoke and he realized he could have hurt her with his ill-conceived plan. "I'm sorry, Sam."

She reached up and kissed him, the butterfly touch going straight to his groin. "I love you, Mac Wanowski."

His heart stuttered. "Sam..."

There was a sudden explosion of sound as the doorway burst open. "RCMP, hands where we can see them." Three uniformed officers entered with choreographed precision, armed and dangerous.

Sam pulled away and took a step toward the police, who turned their guns on her in reaction. She froze. Mac raised his hands and moved in front of her, his mouth dry. "Whoa, take it easy there. We're not going to give you any trouble."

"Please," Sam said, her voice hoarse. "My uncle is having a stroke. He needs help."

One of the men glanced at the one in the center—obviously his superior—and at a short nod, holstered his weapon and strode to Doc, careful to keep a distance between himself and Mac. After a short assessment, he stood. "The sooner he gets medical attention, the better. There's a gun on the bench, sir."

"Understood, Corporal, make the call and start processing the evidence." The sergeant directed them to the sofa. "Have a seat, please. We just need to ask you a few questions while we wait."

Sam wavered, her gaze going to her uncle before she led the way to the couch. Mac took a seat and grasped her hand, giving it a reassuring squeeze.

The sergeant sat in the chair opposite and gave them a piercing stare. "Let's start with your names."

"Mac Wanowski, captain of the Victoria WarHawks." Mac could feel Sam's tension along his side. He wished he could make this easier for her. "Can't we do this later?"

Sergeant Wilkins, according to his nametag, stiffened at his tone, pen poised over his notepad. "Sure. If you'd rather spend time at the precinct, we can arrange that."

It was Sam's turn to squeeze his fingers. "No, it's all right. We'll tell you whatever you want. Mac knows I'm worried about my uncle, that's all. Samantha Walters, physiotherapist. And that's Thomas Edwards, my uncle and the team's doctor."

The sergeant nodded and made some notes. "We're aware of Mr. Edwards. Can you enlighten us as to why you all are in this remote cabin, and why Mr. Edwards seems to be in possession of a firearm?"

Sam met Mac's gaze, her brow furrowed. Much as he wanted to throw Thomas under the bus, he couldn't hurt her that way. "You'll have to ask him when he's recovered. We can't answer that question."

"Can't or won't?" the officer murmured. He flipped

a page in his notepad. "Okay. How about explaining why there was a chair against the door to the den when we arrived, locking you all inside?"

So that's why he couldn't get through. Damnit, Coach. And again, if he wanted to protect Sam, his hands were tied. "I have no idea," he said. True enough. He didn't know why the coach had chosen to risk their lives by locking them in.

"Hmm," Sergeant Wilkens said, tapping the pen against his jaw. "So it has nothing to do with the two men we captured earlier today breaking into a cabin south of here, or one Dan Harris who is currently a guest in one of our patrol cars sitting outside?" He raised a hand before they could answer. "You should know ahead of time, those two men told us a mighty interesting story about your uncle and a gambling syndicate we've been investigating for some time. We take money laundering very seriously in this country, Miss Walters. Unless you want to be charged as an accessory, I suggest you tell us the truth."

Damn, the gloves were off. Mac kissed Sam's brow, aware he might be doing so for the very last time, then turned to the Mountie. "There's no need for that, I'll tell you whatever you want to know."

23

6 MONTHS *later*

MAC LED his team onto the ice at Roger's Arena to the screams of sixteen thousand ravenous fans. They were playing the Vancouver Canucks tonight and it promised to be an exciting game. As they circled the rink, he couldn't help but search the stands for a honey-blond head and cerulean blue eyes, but without much hope. Sam had disappeared.

Both teams formed a line at center ice and waited for the national anthem to begin. There were many things Mac could say he was grateful for; his career, friends, relative health, but it all felt flat. All he could think about was Sam and the last time he's seen her on the courtroom steps. Her uncle had just been convicted of racketeering in collusion with her godfather, Dan Harris. Both men lost their jobs within the NHL and were ordered to pay a restitution of twenty-five thousand dollars plus two years less a day imprisonment. Thanks to a hotshot lawyer team Mac had found and covered the cost on, the sentences were lenient do to the defendants' ages and lack of previous records.

He'd arrived late and sat at the back of the courtroom to watch the proceedings, all the while aching with the need to take Sam's pain away. He didn't think she'd noticed him when it was over and she had walked out holding her crying mother's arm, a young man following close behind, but she'd been waiting on the steps when he exited the building.

"Mac," she'd said, a wealth of emotion in her expressive eyes.

He'd taken her hands, aware her family looked on from the sidewalk below. "How are you, Sam?"

She'd smiled and it had twisted his heart. "Better, thanks to you. It will take time, but I promise we'll pay you back. I can't believe you helped my uncles after..."

"I didn't do it for them," he murmured. "Listen, Sam—"

"Sam, are you coming?" her brother called, his arm wrapped protectively around their mother. The news media were circling like vultures and Mac knew he was running out of time.

She tried to pull away, but he held fast, scared to let her go. "When can I see you again?" he'd demanded, uncaring what the people milling around them thought.

Sam stilled, blue eyes huge in her pale face. "I... I can't. It wouldn't be right. There's too much between us, Mac. You have to see that."

Yeah, he did. He loved her, damnit. He wasn't willing to give up on their relationship. Apparently, *she* didn't feel the same way. He straightened and took a step back, releasing her hands. "Sure, I get it. Don't worry about the money, it was nothing. Take care of yourself, Doc."

Tears pooled and slid down her cheeks unheeded. Mac knew he seemed callous, but he couldn't bring himself to apologize. She was giving up without giving them a chance. He looked down at her family and the anger evaporated. They needed her support right now, he couldn't fault her loyalties, it was one of the many reasons he loved her.

"You better go, they're waiting," he said and leaned down to brush a tender kiss to her lips. Her eyes closed a moment as though to savor his touch, then hurried down the steps and disappeared into the crowd without another word.

That was six months, two days, and five hours ago.

The sportscaster announced the lineup and he took his place, waiting for the puck to drop. The three periods went by at breakneck speed, the Canucks giving them a run for their money, but in the last period the WarHawks took over and scored two goals for the win.

Mac chest bumped his teammates and shook hands with their opponents, then headed off the ice. He wanted to avoid the celebrations, partying just didn't work for him anymore. He glanced up at the fans as he left the rink and froze. Sam stared down at him with a nervous smile.

"Hi," she mouthed.

Mac's heart rocketed around his chest. He dropped his stick and grabbed hold of the top of the wall to lever himself up to her height, his skates searching for purchase against the wood. The spectators watched with avid interest, but that didn't matter—nothing did except that Sam was here. She'd come.

"About time," he said, just before he took her mouth in a ravenous kiss that made the audience hoot and clap.

"I love you," she whispered against his lips.

His chest filled with exhilaration. He'd scored the best trophy of his life—Sam's love.

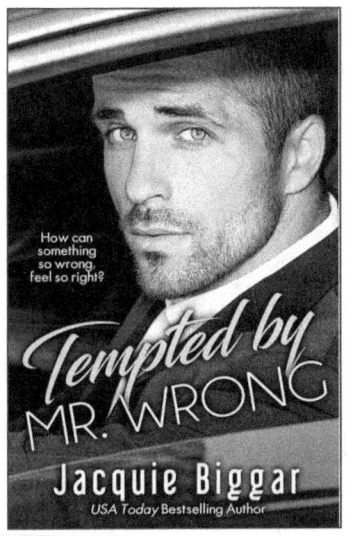

Tammy-Jo woke late after a night spent tossing and turning—and regretting saying no to Jason. Those few moments in the kitchen had replayed in her head for hours. What did he think he was doing, crashing back into their lives and disrupting... everything?

A reporter.

She'd never have figured him for a social media person. He'd always been something of a loner as a teenager. She remembered all the girls totally crushing on him in school—her included. He'd been so different from the normal crowd, with his *keep away* vibe and worn clothes. T.J. hadn't told any of her friends he was her new step-brother. She'd been too embarrassed. And if the truth were told, jealous. The special place she'd occupied in her father's life changed. He brought a woman she didn't know, and wasn't sure she liked, into their home.

And she brought a boy with her.

Seventeen to Tammy-Jo's sweet sixteen, he'd made her young heart pound and secret places grow warm and damp with just a glance from those enigmatic blue eyes. She'd fallen headlong into her first full-blown crush.

It had taken two long years to get Jason into her bed, and only a few short hours to know she'd never be the same again. They'd spent the summer learning everything there was to know about each other—or so she thought—and had planned to move in together while she went to college and he got a job nearby.

When he suddenly left town without explanation,

she'd learned a broken heart does eventually mend. It had taken a while, but she'd gone on to marry Tim and become the society matron her daddy wanted, and she hated.

Now Tim was dead and Jason had returned. Fate was a mean creature.

Even if she wanted to investigate Jason's intentions toward her, and Lord knows she did, there was no way she was going to pull him into the middle of the mess that was her life. He had a good career and friends, while she had...

She looked around the princess bedroom and her mud-splattered clothes from the night before scattered like ugly bruises on the white shag carpet. What if whoever shot Tim came after her? What if the police thought she had something to do with it, as Jason had suggested? Her first instinct was to go running to her father, but pride held her back. It was time she stood on her own two legs. She just hoped they didn't get cut off at the knee.

She glanced at the delicate gold watch on her wrist —a gift from Jason for her eighteenth birthday—and grimaced. Almost eleven a.m.; she was undoubtedly the last to rise. There were bound to be issues she would need to address, not least of which was an explanation of how she'd ended up the laughing stock of the country club yesterday. T.J. had no illusions about how her father would feel about his precious daughter creating such a scene in front of his friends and clients.

Not to mention the dead husband in her front yard.

She showered in record time, but then wasted half an hour trying to find something in her closet that still fit. The pants were too snug—she'd apparently grown hips in the past ten years—and the tops threatened her with indecent exposure. The dirty clothes on the floor might have to do. She sighed and turned to step out of the walk-in closet, then stopped when a ribbon of color caught her eye.

The dress she'd worn the night she convinced Jason to give their relationship a chance.

Could she?

It probably wouldn't even fit.

Jade green and made from the finest silk, everything about the dress screamed seduction from the form-fitting torso, to the sweetheart neckline that showed just the right amount of décolletage to hold a man's attention.

And it had. Jason hadn't taken his eyes off her the whole night. Her heart fluttered. This was crazy. It was only a dress. And she needed something to wear.

T.J. pulled the shimmery material off the hanger and over her head before she changed her mind. The cloth slid down her body like a lover's touch. She smoothed the fabric over her hips and gave a little twist, loving the flirty swish of the skirt just above her knees. Maybe this would give her the confidence boost she was going to need while giving her statement to the police today.

Poor Tim. There'd been no love lost between them, especially towards the end, and even though she'd wished him dead on more than one occasion, she hadn't meant it literally.

Suddenly, the papers she carried in her purse took on a much more sinister perspective. Could they have something to do with Tim's murder?

There was a ringing in her ears and her vision wavered in and out of focus. She put a trembling hand out to brace herself against the wall. Oh, God, what if this was her fault? Maybe, whoever it was had somehow found out the papers were missing, and killed him for it. That was it. Bone deep, she knew she was right.

Which meant she was in a world of trouble.

T.J. stumbled into the other room and searched the floor for her clutch. She was about to panic when she caught sight of it pushed under the edge of her bed. She dropped to her knees, almost hyperventilating, and threw the covers aside so she could grasp the purse. Her fingers shook so hard it was tough getting the clasp undone. But finally, finally she made it, and there they were, folded and hidden in the bottom under her make-up and wallet and glasses and various other odds and ends all women managed to carry in their bags.

She yanked them out, uncaring as her lipstick went rolling into the thick forest of carpet, or that her wallet tumbled from her lap to the floor. She turned and sank onto her bottom, back against the bed, and unfolded the five pages, dreading what she would find.

The first sheet contained some kind of complicated formula. It made no sense to her so she moved on to the next page. Names. Three columns. The first, a garbled —or maybe coded? —version of someone's name. The next held a date and monetary amount. The third? Another date with a total, but this one much higher than the first. What did it mean?

Tim was—had been—a corporate investor, so it made sense that he worked with numbers, but this was different. Secretive. It was written in his handwriting, instead of computer driven, and he'd hidden it away in the back of his safe—the one he thought she didn't know about.

The one she wished now she'd stayed out of.

FREE DOWNLOAD!

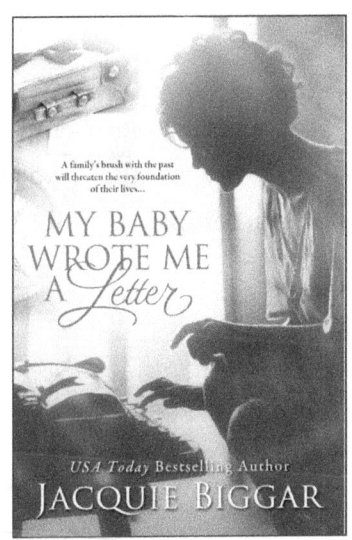

My Baby Wrote Me A Letter

A family's brush with the past will threaten the fabric of their lives.

Eight months pregnant and her Navy husband away on a mission, Grace Freeman craves the security of her childhood home in Canada.

When a letter written by her long-lost mother is found in an old writing desk it creates a tear in the fabric of her family.

Can Grace find a way to bring peace to those she loves, or will a message from the past destroy their future?

Newsletter subscribers also get bonus content and insider information every month. I love giveaways and there is lots of interesting stuff for me to share with you!

Newsletter- Sign up Now!

In 1879 the first organized team, the McGill University Hockey Club, was formed, and with the advent of a basic set of rules, the sport quickly spread across Canada. The first "world championship" was held in 1883 at the Montreal Ice Carnival and was won by McGill. Even though the winter carnival hockey tournament was considered a "world championship," only teams from Eastern Canada participated, according to the Montreal *Gazette*. The first national association, known as the Amateur Hockey Association of Canada, was formed in 1886, with representatives from Québec City, Montréal and Ottawa. A group of colleges, universities, and military and athletic clubs formed the Ontario Hockey Association in 1890. Governor General Lord Stanley donated a trophy in 1893 for the national championship, and the first Stanley Cup game was played 22 March 1893, with Montreal AAA victorious before a crowd of 5000.

Attribution:

https://www.thecanadianencyclopedia.ca/en/article/ice-hockey

ACKNOWLEDGMENTS

Reviews are the lifeblood of any successful author. Without you, we can't be heard.

If you enjoy the story, please consider sharing on your favorite social media sites, as well as GoodReads and from wherever you've bought the book.

Thank you,

Jacquie Biggar

Jacqbiggar.com

JACQUIE BIGGAR is a USA Today bestselling author of Romantic Suspense who loves to write about tough, alpha males and strong, contemporary women willing to show their men that true power comes from love.

She is the author of the popular Wounded Hearts series and has just started a new series in paranormal suspense, Mended Souls.

She has been blessed with a long, happy marriage and enjoys writing romance novels that end with happily-ever-afters.

Jacquie lives in paradise along the west coast of

Canada with her family and loves reading, writing, and flower gardening. She swears she can't function without coffee, preferably at the beach with her sweetheart. :)

Sign up now to keep up with Jacquie's new releases, excerpts, giveaways, and more:

Newsletter

jacqbiggar.com
jbiggar@jacqbiggar.com

facebook.com/jacqbiggar

twitter.com/jacqbiggar

instagram.com/jacqbiggar

amazon.com/author/jacquiebiggar

bookbub.com/authors/jacquie-biggar

WOUNDED HEARTS SERIES

Tidal Falls

The Rebel's Redemption

Twilight's Encore

The Sheriff Meets His Match

Summer Lovin'

Wounded Hearts Box Set

Maggie's Revenge

With This Heart

MENDED SOULS SERIES

The Guardian

The Beast Within

GAMBLING HEARTS

Hold 'Em

Crazy Little Thing Called Love

BLUE HAVEN

Sweetheart Cove

SINGLE TITLES

Silver Bells

The Lady Said No

My Baby Wrote Me A Letter

Tempted by Mr. Wrong

Valentine: A Hearts and Kisses Romance

Mistletoe Inn

Skating on Thin Ice